Pem J 11-07

W9-DJA-527

PEMBERVILLE
PUBLIC LIBRARY
375 E. FRONT ST
GENERAL DELIVERY
PEMBERVILLE, OH 43450-9999

Getting to First Base

with Danalda Chase

MATT BEAM

DUTTON CHILDREN'S BOOKS

DUTTON CHILDREN'S BOOKS

A division of Penguin Young Readers Group

Published by the Penguin Group

Penguin Group (USA) Inc., 375 Hudson Street, New York, New York 10014, U.S.A. / Penguin Group (Canada), 90 Eglinton Avenue East, Suite 700, Toronto, Ontario, Canada M4P 2Y3 (a division of Pearson Penguin Canada Inc.) / Penguin Books Ltd, 80 Strand, London WC2R 0RL, England / Penguin Ireland, 25 St Stephen's Green, Dublin 2, Ireland (a division of Penguin Books Ltd) / Penguin Group (Australia), 250 Camberwell Road, Camberwell, Victoria 3124, Australia (a division of Pearson Australia Group Pty Ltd / Penguin Books India Pvt Ltd, 11 Community Centre, Panchsheel Park, New Delhi - 110 017, India / Penguin Group (NZ), Cnr Airborne and Rosedale Roads, Albany, Auckland 1310, New Zealand (a division of Pearson New Zealand Ltd) / Penguin Books (South Africa) (Pty) Ltd, 24 Sturdee Avenue, Rosebank, Johannesburg 2196, South Africa / Penguin Books Ltd, Registered Offices: 80 Strand, London WC2R 0RL, England

This book is a work of fiction. Names, characters, places, and incidents are either the product of the author's imagination or are used fictitiously, and any resemblance to actual persons, living or dead, business establishments, events, or locales is entirely coincidental.

Copyright © 2007 by Matt Beam

All rights reserved. No part of this publication may be reproduced or transmitted in any form or by any means, electronic or mechanical, including photocopying, recording, or any information storage and retrieval system now known or to be invented, without permission in writing from the publisher, except by a reviewer who wishes to quote brief passages in connection with a review written for inclusion in a magazine, newspaper, or broadcast.

The publisher does not have any control over and does not assume any responsibility for author or third-party websites or their content.

CIP Data is available.

Published in the United States by Dutton Children's Books,
a division of Penguin Young Readers Group
345 Hudson Street, New York, New York 10014
www.penguin.com/youngreaders

Designed by Heather Wood
Printed in USA / First Edition
ISBN 978-0-525-47578-1
1 3 5 7 9 10 8 6 4 2

To Lorraine

◆

Acknowledgments: I want to thank my parents, the four of them, for the many ways they each helped me become the writer I am today. I also want to thank the rest of my family, my friends, and my supporters, especially Michelle for her eyes, ears, and insight. I want to thank my editor, Sarah Shumway, for her support and guidance throughout this remarkable process. And of course, I want to thank Lorraine, for everything.

CONTENTS

THE LINEUP

NAME: Darcy Spillman (me)
POSITION: Third Base
GAMES PLAYED: 46
CAREER BATTING AVERAGE: .263
#1 GIRL: Danalda Chase
CAREER HIGHLIGHT:
Inside-the-park, three-error single/home run for the Twins in the last inning to win a quarter-final in Cherrydale Little League Baseball last year.
QUOTE: "The only thing better than a great baseball player is one who doesn't act like he knows it."

3B

Darcy Spillman

Ralph Peterson

NAME: Ralph Peterson
POSITION: Pitcher
GAMES PLAYED: 42
CAREER BATTING AVERAGE: .322
#1 GIRL: Simone Smith
CAREER HIGHLIGHT:
Taking off his catching equipment for the Angels last year and taking the mound for the first time in his career to strike out five in a row to win a regular-season game.
QUOTE: "Just you wait and see. Simone will be a sizzler."

NAME: Dwight Middlebury
POSITION: Shortstop
GAMES PLAYED: 47
CAREER BATTING AVERAGE: .149
#1 GIRL: No one
CAREER HIGHLIGHT:
When he took a pitch to the head in last spring's semifinal playoffs, scoring the winning run for the Tigers.
QUOTE: "Nothing—absolutely nothing—is more important than baseball."

Dwight Middlebury

Danalda Chase

NAME: Danalda Chase
POSITION: First Base
GAMES PLAYED: Unknown
CAREER BATTING AVERAGE: 1.000
(1 for 1)
#1 GUY: Unknown
CAREER HIGHLIGHT:
Getting the most beautiful
single I've ever seen in my life.
QUOTE: "Um . . . excuse me . . .
do you know where Room 208
is?"

NAME: Sam Spillman
(my mother)
POSITION: Center Field
GAMES PLAYED: 1
CAREER BATTING AVERAGE: .000
#1 GUY: Nap (my dad)
CAREER HIGHLIGHT:
Missing every pitch ever thrown
to her.
QUOTE: "I didn't get a hit, but I
did a nice braid of Jane Smythe's
hair on the bench in the third
inning."

Sam Spillman

2B

Joseph Spillman

NAME: Joseph Spillman (my grandpa)

POSITION: Second Base (for most of his career)

GAMES PLAYED: 587

CAREER BATTING AVERAGE: .221

#1 GIRL: Rose Spillman (my grandma)

CAREER HIGHLIGHT: Driving in the winning run for the minor league team, the Haliburton Herons, to win a playoff game.

QUOTE (THERE ARE THOUSANDS): "Throw the gall-stoned ball!"

NAME: Nap Spillman (my dad)

POSITION: Right Field

GAMES PLAYED: 11

CAREER BATTING AVERAGE: "Not very good." (according to him)

#1 GIRL: "Your mother, of course."

CAREER HIGHLIGHT: According to Grandpa Spillman, "I'm sorry to say there's not one single highlight."

QUOTE: "I care more about your 'academic' average, Darcy."

RF

Nap Spillman

NAME: Beatrice "Beattie" Spillman (my sister)
POSITION: Catcher
GAMES PLAYED: 25
CAREER BATTING AVERAGE: .774
#1 GUY: Floyd Flemington
CAREER HIGHLIGHT: (There are tons!) One amazing throw-out at second and a grand slam home run for the Sox in her first-ever softball game.
QUOTE: "Sure, I'll play catch with you . . . but only because you're my brother."

Beatrice "Beattie" Spillman

NAME: Kamna Singh
POSITION: Left Field ("Way outfield. Like, not on it.")
GAMES PLAYED: 0
CAREER BATTING AVERAGE: "What? Are you kidding?"
#1 GUY: "Guys are impossible. So, I guess none."
CAREER HIGHLIGHT: Telling her mom in fifth grade that playing softball was "about the last thing I want to do."
QUOTE: "The only thing worse than baseball is cricket."

Kamna Singh

1

◆

BASEBALL IS LIFE

◆

a single **def.** A hit that allows a batter to safely get to first base.

"I can't believe the World Series is over," I said, looking up at the sky as I sat between my two best friends near the school baseball diamond.

"Yeah, and I can't believe the Yankees won again!" Dwight said, smacking his forehead.

"Well, *I* can't believe Danalda Chase is about to step to the plate!" Ralph declared, pointing a freckled finger in front of him.

I leveled my eyes across the field. On the first-base line, waiting to bat, was Danalda Chase, one of the cutest girls at Cherrydale

Junior High. I didn't really know Danalda because she'd gone to Newton Primary, not Burton like the three of us, but somehow it seemed strange that she was playing baseball—she wasn't exactly the sporty type. Danalda was talking to a friend, curling the hair that had escaped from her ponytail over her ear, not really paying attention to the play. It looked like a few girls had rallied a game and dragged in a few who normally wouldn't play.

"Who cares about Danalda?" Dwight snapped, throwing his skinny arms in the air. "We were talking about the Yankees and—"

"*Darcy* cares about Danalda," Ralph interrupted, nudging me with his elbow. "Don't you, Darce?"

"What're you talking about?" I said, unable to take my eyes away from the diamond. "I barely even know her."

"Like that matters! You are so bit, Darce," Ralph yelped, throwing his legs up with laughter. "Excuse me, Doctor, I think this boy has got a fever. . . ."

"Shut up, will you?" I said. "She's on deck now."

"I can't believe this conversation," Dwight said.

"Believe it," Ralph said. "If you hadn't noticed, Dwighty boy, we're in junior high now. And you know what that means!"

"No. What?" Dwight said.

"That Danalda Chase, and all the rest of the girls we know, are now *junior high girls*," Ralph said. "Take smokin' Simone Smith, for example."

"Simone?" Dwight squealed. "Don't you mean *Simon*?"

"Look at her!" Ralph argued, pointing again to the end of the batting line where Simone was standing. "She is definitely no longer *Simon*, and besides, she's in the Cool Crowd."

It was true—something had happened to Simone when she'd visited her aunt and uncle in California last summer. Suddenly she looked like she was in ninth grade—her hair longer and her body suddenly becoming more like a woman's. Ralph had flipped when he saw her in September.

"Cool Crowd?" Dwight exclaimed. "Jeez, can't we just get back to talking about baseball—"

"Guys," I complained, "will you be quiet for a second?"

There was a moment of silence, and then Dwight spoke softly. "I'm just . . . I'm just very disappointed in you two."

"Look," I said as I saw Danalda preparing to bat, "she's showing classic on-deck symptoms!"

"You're not kidding," Ralph agreed. "She can barely hold on to the bat."

Again Ralph was right. When you're "on deck," it's like sitting in a roller-coaster car slowly going up the first big hill. There's no turning back. Your heart begins to pound in your chest. You fidget. You watch the current batter like the car ahead. Practice swings help with the butterflies, but Danalda was a true nervous rookie, balancing the bat between her fingertips and the ground, never lifting it up for practice or distraction. The batter ahead of Danalda popped up to the pitcher. She gave one more desperate look at her friends, who were giggling. I couldn't look away.

Danalda hit her bat lightly onto home plate, raised it over her shoulder, and transformed. Her hands were not choked up like most newbies, but well placed near the end of the shaft, and she held it at a nice forty-five-degree angle. She even waggled the bat a bit, in small slow circles. Her friends stopped giggling and watched as Andrea Kraft threw a juicy first pitch. Danalda took a magnificent swing. She smacked a drive between second and third base for one of the most beautiful singles I've ever seen in my life. When she arrived on first base, then shrugged at her friends, I was pretty sure she had no idea that she was my newest Most Valuable Player.

"Danalda Chase, what a hitter!" Ralph said as we walked back to our seventh grade classes at the end of lunch. "You heard about how she got to first base with Vernon Maxwell, didn't you?"

"When?" I said. "Not today—Danalda was very alone when she arrived at first base."

"No, not that first base!" Ralph exclaimed. "*First base* first base!"

"But Vernon has an injured hamstring from track, and Danalda barely ever—"

"No, you nut-bar, first base, like—"

"The white, square bag ninety feet from home plate," Dwight said, making a shape of a base with his two index fingers and thumbs.

"No," Ralph said, throwing his head back in frustration.

"Sheesh! How did I get stuck with you two losers? First base like—"

"Ralph!" Mr. Givens's deep, distinctive voice bellowed across the field. "More walking and less talking. Shut it and shake it."

"Like—"

"Ralph!" he bellowed again. "What part of 'Shut it and shake it' didn't you understand?"

Ralph shrugged and picked up the pace. As we got closer to the building, he looked over and whispered over to me emphatically, "Danalda and Vernon made out!"

I thought about this for a second.

"You mean they kissed?" I whispered back.

Ralph nodded.

"But you said they got to first base."

"That's what 'getting to first base' means, you idiot!" he said.

"Ralph!" Mr. Givens yelled. "I'm *not* going to ask you again."

Ralph, Dwight, and I moved quickly, stepping into line and filing in through the school doors.

The only conversation I've ever had with Danalda was when she asked me how to find Room 208 on the first day of school, and it wasn't exactly a conversation. All I could muster was a weak smile and a finger pointed down the hall. So for next the couple of days after Danalda's beautiful swing, I began secretly checking her out at school, trying to figure out what this "getting to first base" kiss was all about.

I now understood that some people treated a kiss like Ralph, Dwight, and I treated a nice single at the diamond, but it wasn't like she was strutting around the school grounds with her Championship Make Out T-shirt and cap on, bragging about her big kiss. To top it all off, I never ever saw Vernon and Danalda hanging out together. What was going on?

Once I started checking Danalda out, though, I couldn't stop. Along with beautiful bluish-gray eyes and sleek blond hair, Danalda had this calm shyness about her. I had heard from other kids who went to Newton that Danalda was one of the meanest girls in our class, but I just couldn't believe it. Unlike other cool girls like Jennifer Crumble, Danalda's best friend, who turned up their noses as they passed you in the hallway, Danalda looked down and away as if she just didn't want to bother you. Danalda was the only cute girl who made me feel like I actually had a chance.

A couple of weeks later, Dwight, Ralph, and I still had not given up on baseball. We were taking advantage of a warmer-than-normal Saturday afternoon in November. After hours playing catch, the three of us sat down on the bleachers.

"I definitely think Darcy should go for Danalda Chase this winter," Ralph said out of blue.

"Huh?" I said, trying to act nonchalant.

"What are you talking about, Ralphy-boy?" Dwight needled in his high-pitched voice, tossing the ball up in the air.

"Really, guys!" Ralph exclaimed. "I mean, the baseball season is long gone and our careers are basically finished—the junior high team will be impossible to make next spring."

The three of us had completed our final year of Little League last spring. I played on the Twins, and we got knocked out in the quarterfinals. Ralph's Angels and Dwight's Tigers played against one another in the semis, when Dwight took a pitch to the head to force in the winning run. In the finals, Dwight went 0 for 4, and they lost 6–1 to the Cubs.

"So," Ralph continued, smirking. "It's the beginning of a new part of our lives: meet a nice girl, get married, and start a family."

Dwight laughed, standing up. "Sometimes I really think you are crazier than me."

"Yeah," I said, pulling at my hat. "What the heck are you talking about?"

"Do I have to repeat myself?" Ralph said. "Okay, I will. I think Darcy should go for Danalda. Wake up, guys. Junior high girls are waiting for us to make our move."

"Danalda Chase," Dwight jumped in, "is one of the prettiest girls at school. I mean, getting her to go out with Darcy—sorry, Darce—would be impossible. It would be like getting a hit off Roger Clemens or Tom Seaver or Sandy Koufax—"

"Exactly my point," Ralph said, sitting up suddenly. "That's the thing. The great Yankee Joe DiMaggio married Marilyn Monroe, one of the sexiest women ever, and I mean he was a good-looking guy and all, but it was the baseball that got him the girl. Once he lost his baseball, she split like a cracked bat."

"That's not exactly how it happened," Dwight interjected.

"Who cares?" Ralph said, waving Dwight off. "Let's face it. As soon as next spring comes along and we *don't* make the Cheetahs, we are nothin' but three guys talking about baseball. Until then we might as well use our status as real baseball players—or in Dwight's case, a really bad baseball player—to get some girls."

"Whatever," Dwight said, ignoring Ralph's insult. "All I care about is practicing my fielding against my basement wall all winter, watching my hitting videos, and impressing the heck out of Coach Rizzuto next spring."

Coach Rizzuto was the coach of the Cheetahs, the junior high team, and even though Dwight loved baseball, he was truly terrible at it.

"Jeez, can't you get your mind off of baseball for a second?" Ralph asked. "And didn't you notice how far Darcy's mouth dropped when Danalda was at bat the other week?"

"Whatever," I said, blushing.

"Remember," he said. "Ballplayers always get the girl . . . and they don't call it getting to first base for nothin'."

"What *are* you talking about?" Dwight demanded.

"Actually," Ralph said, smirking, "I'm really not sure, but it sounds good anyway."

"You're nuts," I said.

"Yeah, that's Yogi Berra logic," Dwight said, agreeing with me.

"Yogi Berra was the ultimate baseball player," Ralph stated.

"But he wasn't even close to the *best* baseball player," Dwight quipped.

"Says the guy who's never broken the .150 batting barrier!" Ralph retorted.

"Says the guy who still has trouble working out his average!" Dwight sneered.

"Not this again," I said. But I didn't mean it. In primary school, we talked about baseball every second of the day, but now in seventh grade, cliques, clothing, harder homework, and girls were getting in the way.

After tossing the ball around a bit more, the three of us went our separate ways. As I walked home alone, I couldn't get this whole "getting to first base" business out of my head. Maybe Ralph was right: I had to take advantage of my baseball player status while I still had it. If "getting to first base" meant kissing a girl, then maybe the rest of my baseball knowledge could help me out with girls. I wondered what a check swing translated to. Or a foul ball. I did know that I couldn't seem to get Danalda off my mind. How do you start going after a girl, anyway? Maybe baseball was my answer. If anyone would know something about this, I thought, it would be my grandpa. He would definitely be able to help me figure out what girls and baseball had in common.

2

◆

WHEN LIFE THROWS YOU SPITBALLS

◆

spitball **def.** When the pitcher manipulates the ball with spit, or any other slippery substance, so that his pitches have unpredictable movement. It is an illegal pitch.

When I was really little, my grandpa came to all of my games. At the diamond, he always sat in his lawn chair on the third-base line with his red plastic visor pulled down almost over his eyes, one elbow on the arm of the chair, and his hand stuck on his chin. Whenever he spoke, he barely lifted his head, but you sure could hear what he said. When we walked home together, there was also no mistaking Grandpa's feelings. He trailed along excitedly, telling me exactly what he was sure I was thinking at the plate.

"The count was zero and one, and you're thinking, this is my pitch."

When I first started playing, every pitch was my pitch. Unfortunately, the ball didn't always feel the same way.

"There's a guy on first and no outs, so you are thinking about advancing the runner."

I was thinking about hitting it. A foul ball. A pop-up. A mere tick. Anything.

"You decide to wait on it and slap it into left field."

I used to insist on using a too-big bat, and was *always* late on pitches.

"And you got yourself a single, advanced the runner to second, and you're two for three on the day. You're now batting about .500. Not bad for a kid your size. I've always said the Spillmans were meant to play ball! Well, maybe not Nap."

My dad—Nap, as everyone in our family calls him—has never been into baseball. You might even say he just doesn't like it. Whenever I come back from a game, Nap *does* always ask me how it went, but I can tell by the look on his face that he's barely listening. My grandpa, on the other hand, has always been super-supportive about my game. When I was younger, after I came back from the diamond he would immediately come up to my room with me, pull out a sheet from my desk drawer, and help me work out my average. Beattie, my little sister, always followed us upstairs and sat on my bed until we'd finished the calculations. At first I'd only add slashes to night and season's totals and Grandpa would do the division. Then he got me to write out the equations for him. "Okay, move the three down there. That's right. Now, how many times do you think five goes into thirty?"

Beattie is the best baseball player in my family, and she's only nine. When she was two, Beattie was still too small to swing my blue plastic bat, but she would drag it around the house all day long. In our early family photos, Beattie is always sucking her right thumb and gripping the bat in her other hand. Her first-ever swing was a good hard one that hit me in the stomach as she tried to keep me from taking it from her. When Beattie was old enough for T-ball, she could already hit one of my softer, overhand pitches.

Nap and Sam, my mom, sent Beattie to Newton Primary because they have a great girls' softball team. My parents are a little out of it when it comes to my baseball career, but they always treat Beattie's skills like they are a set of amazing, unending scientific discoveries. I guess I can't blame them—they *are* both science professors at a small college. Grandpa wasn't at all surprised by Beattie's baseball skills, or her choice of catcher as a position.

"She's the spitting image of Grandma Rose," he said. "Except Grandma had a better throw to second."

Grandma Rose died when I was in kindergarten, so I never saw her throw a baseball. My memories of her are few—I remember her funny-smelling flowery dresses and a crackly, soothing voice.

Our photo albums are filled with her smile, and the old black-and-white family photo has been on the mantel over our fireplace since I can remember. The way that Grandma Rose holds her head up and spreads a smile across her face makes me wish I could remember her better.

When I got home after playing with my two friends, I found Grandpa standing in the middle of the living room.

"Hi, Grandpa," I said. "What are you doing?"

"Oh, hey there, Darce," he said. "I was just . . . just . . . stretching my . . . um . . . legs." He paused. "Were you throwing the ball around?"

"Yeah, with Ralph and Dwight."

"Big Mouth and Skin-and-Bones, right?"

"Yep," I said, laughing and flopping on the sofa across from him. "That's pretty much them."

"So," he said. "When do your tryouts start?"

"Tryouts? It's almost winter, Grandpa. The season's long over. Tryouts aren't for, like, five months."

Grandpa suddenly winced like his head hurt. "Oh, right, right."

Then his eyes changed. "You shoulda thrown the ball, you know."

"I did. Tons of times today."

His eyes were focused above my head like I wasn't there.

"No," he said sternly. "I always told you, Nap. Don't think, just throw it. Just throw the *gall-stoned* ball. Why couldn't you just do that?"

"Grandpa, it's me, Darcy," I said, startled.

"Darcy . . . Dar-cy," he said, confused like he hadn't heard the word before.

"Are you okay, Grandpa?" I asked, leaning forward on the sofa.

He sat down beside me and didn't say anything for a minute.

I was about to get up when Grandpa shook his head and grunted. He turned to me, his eyes alive again. Then he bent toward me secretly and whispered, "Did I ever tell you about Al 'Spitball' Zimer?"

"I don't think so," I said, seeing that he'd returned to his old self.

"Well, I should've," Grandpa said, shaking his head. "Yep, that guy was a *gall-stoned* sneaky bugger. Never ever knew when one of those pitches was coming."

Ex–Yankee catcher and coach Yogi Berra once said, "All pitchers are liars or crybabies." Grandpa agreed with this idea, especially the liar part, and he made sure I never even tried out for the position. Still, Grandpa liked to tell stories about the best players in baseball history, some of whom were pitchers. One of his favorite tales was about the most famous spitball pitcher, Gaylord Perry.

Perry spent twenty-two years of his Hall of Fame career throwing the spitball, getting caught only once. Perry apparently used jelly or Vaseline to manipulate the ball, hiding some under his cap, glove, or belt. Or so everyone thought. Truth be told, the umpires weren't sure where he was hiding it. Perry's pitches would dive in midair as if rolling off a table.

Grandpa spoke about spitballers the way Mrs. Soldier, my sixth-grade teacher, talked about pirates. *Yes, they were evil and greedy, but they were darned good at what they did.* Grandpa also told stories about his days in the minor leagues, all the unusual characters that never made it to the majors. But before that afternoon, I was sure I had never heard the name Al "Spitball" Zimer.

3

THE STATS
ARE EVERYTHING

stats **def.** This is a short form for "baseball statistics." Baseball has a long history and an even longer list of stats. To some baseball fans, the stats are everything, especially during the winter.

"What's up, Darceman?" Ralph said, leaning on my locker at the end of the first Monday in December.

"Not much," I said.

"Have you made your move on Danalda yet?"

"Um . . . no," I said. "Not yet."

"Let's go talk to her now," he said, standing on his tiptoes. "She's right over there with Simone."

"No," I whispered to Ralph. "Cut it out. I've got to go home and . . . study."

The truth was I had to go home to take care of Grandpa. Everyone, even Beattie, had noticed that he was acting pretty scatterbrained. He misplaced his glasses almost every day, and twice he made a sandwich in the kitchen and then forgot to eat it. Every once in a while, Grandpa couldn't remember words that you just couldn't forget, like *chair*, or *shoe*, or *Darcy*. It was weird. And because it was December, Nap and Sam were preparing for exams at the college in the afternoons, so they gave me the job of coming home to make sure Grandpa was okay.

"Fine," Ralph said, moving off toward the girls. "But you'd better make your move soon. You never know when it'll be too late."

When I got home, I was happy to find Grandpa settled into his favorite seat in the den with a newspaper on his lap.

"Hey, Darce," he said. "Not out with Dwight and the other one, Big Mouth, what's his name?"

"Ralph," I said, laughing. "No. I'm staying in—it's too cold out anyway, and I've got a ton of studying to do later on."

"Right, right," he said, smiling. Grandpa didn't know I was coming home to care for him. "Glad I don't have to do homework anymore."

"Yeah," I said, sitting down.

"Tough time of the year, eh, Darce?" he said, raising his eyebrows. "I always said, 'Winter's hell for the baseball player.'"

I nodded. "I can't wait till spring."

Grandpa cast his eye over his newspaper.

"Grandpa," I said shyly.

"Yes, Darcy."

"Does baseball, kind of, in a way, have anything to do with, in a sort of weird way with—"

"Speak your mind, Darcy," he interrupted. "Hesitators always strike out."

I collected myself for a moment.

"Does liking a girl have anything to do with . . . um . . . baseball?"

Grandpa's eyes widened like a goldfish's. He reached over for a rushed slurp of his tea.

"The question is an interesting one," he said softly. "Baseball and love, or liking a girl, in your case, have everything to do with each other. Everything." He beamed at me. "You know how I met your grandma?"

I nodded in a way that said I wanted to hear it again.

"You remember Dermott Brokoski, right?" he said.

"Best catching arm you've ever seen."

"You bet your gall-stoned business!" Grandpa declared as he wagged his finger at me. "Dermott was also the one who made the connection between love and baseball. You see, Dermott was my best friend on the Haliburton Herons, and he was the best fielding catcher that I'd ever played with. The problem was he couldn't hit a baseball for love nor money.

"But," Grandpa said, smiling, "he was the most superstitious player I ever met! He stuffed his left back pocket with hay, had only coffee and lollipops before day games, and only steak and eggs at noon to prepare for night games. At the plate, he went from kissing the bat to spitting on it. He chewed his gum on the left side of his mouth, then the right. He played with his socks high and tight on the weekends and day games, then wrinkled and saggy like an elephant's ankles at night. And—"

"What about baseball and love?" I said impatiently.

"Just hold your horses," Grandpa said, lifting up his hand. "I'm getting to that, Darce."

Grandpa shifted and settled into the story. "Okay. It was a Thursday night, and we'd just won a game against the Collingwood Cardinals. The whole team went to McSweeney's Bar and Grill. We used to call it McSweeney's Charred and Spilled, for the not-so-hot food and service. Anyway, I was always looking for the woman of my dreams, and I spotted a couple of young ladies in the corner of the room, sitting away from the rest of the restaurant. One of them had a sparkle in her eye that I couldn't resist."

"Grandma," I said, entranced.

Grandpa nodded and continued. "I stepped forward. 'I'm Joseph Spillman,' I said. 'And this is Dermott Brokoski, and we were wondering if we could order you a soda.'

"Your grandma smirked.

"This is Ms. Prine and I'm Ms. Broach,' she said. 'And you can sit down if you make it *two* sodas, but only for the time it takes us to drink them down.'

"We sat down and ordered the drinks. Pressed for time, I starting talking up a storm. Boy, could I talk back then. I went on and on about baseball and how good we had been that night. That Ms. Prine, she had a sharp tongue. And she wasn't interested in baseball, one wink.

"But I could tell that your grandma was interested," Grandpa said, smiling. "Dermott, he was shy about girls. He wasn't saying a thing.

"Then," he continued, leaning back and staring at the ceiling. "I don't know why I said it to this day, I guess I was desperate to get through to your grandma before she finished her soda. I said, 'I bet you and I were meant to be together from here to eternity.' I decided to swing for the fences, Darce. That's what I was good at.

"Well," Grandpa said, his eyes getting wide again. "I was expecting your grandma to be embarrassed, but she simply raised her eyebrows at me and said, 'Is that so, Mr. Spillman? Why don't you prove it, then?'

"Ms. Prine squealed and hit the table with her hands like she just got a ticket to the show. 'I think we have a challenge on our hands!' she said.

"This got Dermott squirming in his seat, excited. He liked anything that had to do with games and superstition.

"'Okay, okay,' he said. 'This is my area of expertise. Let's see now, Ms. Broach. Um . . . what's your favorite number?'

"'Nine,' your grandma said without hesitation.

"'Perfect,' I said, winking at Dermott. 'Nine players on the field. She's a baseball fan.'

"Ms. Prine guffawed, and your grandma just shrugged. She was finally blushing a bit, and I couldn't take my eyes off her.

"'All right, Spillsie,' Dermott said. "What's *your* favorite color?'

"'You know it's red, Derm. It's our team color,' I answered.

"Dermott nodded.

"'What's your first name?' he said to her.

"Your grandma stared cold. 'Rose,' she said.

"'A good guess!' Dermott said, hooting, and clapped his hands. 'Red rose. Now if that's not romantic, I don't know what is!'

"Ms. Prine shook her head in disbelief, and I tried to swallow down the lump that was growing in my throat.

"'All right,' Dermott said, not wanting to lose momentum. 'Last question, then it's sealed: eternity for the two of you.'

"Your grandma and I both shifted in our seats.

"'When's your birthday?' Dermott asked.

"'February twenty-first," she said.

"'What year?'

"'None of your beeswax, Mr. Brokoski.'

"Dermott leaned back and put his hand through his hair. He stared at that ceiling for the longest minute of my life.

"All of sudden, Dermott asked for a pen. Ms. Prine had one in her purse. Dermott grabbed it and started scribbling on a napkin. After a minute, he looked up at me like he'd just discovered insulin. He shoved the napkin in front of me.

"'Is this your current batting average?'

"I hadn't done my totals for the game that night, so I went through Dermott's calculations quickly. It looked right, but I felt pressed for time. I nodded my head.

"Dermott looked over at your grandma with the gravest face you've ever seen. He said, 'You were born in the second month on the twenty-first. Read the batting average circled on that napkin.'

"Your grandma turned the napkin around. She let out a sigh.

"'Two-twenty-one.'

"And from that time, your grandma Rose and I quickly fell in love. By the end of the summer, we were as good as glued to each other."

After the story, Grandpa was tired. He asked me if I could read to him from one of his favorite books about the greatest baseball teams in history. I got out the book, and Grandpa closed his eyes, putting his head back on his chair. I had been reading out loud for a while, and I thought he had fallen asleep when all of a sudden he lurched forward with his eyes wide open.

"Did I ever tell you about Al 'Spitball' Zimer?"

"Yeah, Grandpa, in the living room the other day."

"I did, didn't I," he said uncertainly. "Well, anyway, he's a *gall-stoned* sneaky one, I'll tell ya. You never know when one of those spitballs is coming."

4

◆

TRAINING IN THE OFF-SEASON

◆

winter ball **def.** During the winter, some baseball pros head south and play for teams in the Caribbean to keep their game sharp.

Nap isn't crazy about baseball at the best of times, but during the Christmas break, when he was in the middle of marking exams, it was clear he simply wasn't happy about us playing catch with our new equipment *inside*.

"Darcy! Beattie!" he yelled down the stairs. "Stop throwing the baseball down there. Go outside and play. It's not *that* cold out. I need silence . . . for at least an hour."

Beattie and I were restless. We were both going through baseball withdrawal, and our friends were away. Her best friend,

Laura, was in Florida for the Christmas break, and both Ralph and Dwight were visiting relatives out of town.

"I'm not going to get my new glove wet before next season," I said. "Let's go to Cirelli's instead."

Cirelli's was a corner store a couple of blocks away from our house. We killed some time on the walk pitching snowballs to each other, using our hands as bats. When we stepped into Cirelli's, Dave Vrbata, a guy from my grade, was looking through a basketball magazine from the rack.

"Hey, Darcy," he said, looking up as we kicked the snow off our boots. "Are you going to Andrea's party?"

"What party?" I said.

"Yeah," Beattie said, looking up at Dave. "What party?"

Dave laughed at Beattie. "It's tonight at eight. Andrea told me to tell anyone from school who wasn't away on vacation."

"Are there going to be parents there?" Beattie asked. "Otherwise I don't think—"

"Beattie!" I snarled.

"I'm just saying," Beattie said, moving off to buy us some licorice.

"So what's the deal?" I asked, finally turning to Dave.

"Her parents are going to be there," Dave admitted. "But she's got this great basement, and the door will be closed. It should be pretty cool."

"Who's going?" I asked casually. I was secretly hoping he'd say Danalda.

Dave shrugged and smiled. "I know Andrea will be there. Oh yeah, and Zoë Turnbull, Greg Harwood and Thelma, I think."

"Cool," I said. I didn't really know Greg or Zoë, but I'd known Thelma since preschool when she took off her shoes, used her toes to fingerpaint, and managed to track bright pink footprints all over the classroom. Thelma was nice, but I'd never really hung out with her. Dave played hoops, not baseball, and Andrea had never been in my class, but I knew them both well enough that I thought it would be fun. Besides, you can only spend so much time with your little sister.

"Sure," I said. "Sounds good."

"Yeah, but we'll have ask our parents," Beattie said, suddenly again only a few feet away with a bag full of licorice.

"Beattie!" I exclaimed, stepping to chase her as she whipped out of the store.

"Little sisters," I said to Dave, and followed Beattie out the door.

At dinner that night, I told my parents about Andrea's party, and Sam immediately demanded, "Will there be parents present?"

"Yes," Beattie answered for me as I glared at her across the table. "But Darcy and his friends will be in the basement. It has a door, which is going to be locked. So the parents can't—"

"That's enough, Beattie," Sam said. She looked over at Nap. "It sounds fine to me, Darcy. Do you want a ride?"

"It's just a couple of blocks away," I said, getting up to clear my dishes. "I'll call when I'm on my way home."

An hour later, I was walking to Andrea's house. As I neared her place, I started to worry and wonder what I would do if Danalda was there. Ever since my conversation with Grandpa, I was pretty sure there was a connection between love and baseball, but if baseball was going to be the key to my success with Danalda, how would I start? Maybe my career batting average would help me as it did with Grandpa. It was .263, which couldn't be Danalda's birthday—there weren't sixty-three days in a month. Maybe her street number was 263, or 263 were the first three digits of her phone number. Maybe it would be different with us. Maybe, I thought hopefully, I could just start talking to her about baseball, and everything would just fall into place.

I was thinking these thoughts as I knocked on Andrea's door. Her mother let me in, I took off my jacket and boots, and she pointed me to the basement door. I walked slowly down the stairs, still worrying about whether Danalda would be there or not. I heard the chatter of a bunch of people and I held my breath. When I reached the last step, I scanned the room.

Danalda was nowhere to be seen, but there was a pop bottle in the middle of a circle of boys and girls. Dave had forgotten to mention one important detail: this was a spin-the-bottle party.

I didn't think anyone had noticed my arrival. I turned to escape back up the stairs when I felt a hand on my leg through the banister.

"Where do you think you're going?" Thelma asked, laughing.

Before I could respond, she told me, "You're going nowhere fast, that's where. Now get down here."

I cautiously turned and took a step down the stairs.

"Hey," she said. "Is that a new sweater?"

"Yeah, I got it for Christmas."

"Nice. What else did you get?"

"Um . . . a new baseball glove," I replied as Dave nodded to me from across the room. I was trapped.

"A new glove?" she said as I reached the bottom of the stairs. "That's pretty cool."

"Yeah, I guess," I said, stepping down the remaining stairs. "I've been using the same glove for years. It was actually my dad's from way back in the dark ages, but it was barely used because he, like, basically hates baseball. I didn't want to use it at first, but my grandpa would have none of that. He said, 'It's the hand that's inside the glove that matters.' Now it's hard to get used to using something else."

Thelma smiled. She's always been funny in a kind of goofy way, and she's one of those people who always seems happy. I suppose that's why when Andrea suddenly called us all to the spin-the-bottle circle, she just couldn't stop happily gabbing away.

"I've played baseball before," she said as we moved toward the circle. "Or softball, I mean. What's the difference again? I was six years old, and my team was called the Hankees."

"You mean the Yankees?"

"Oh, right." She giggled. "The Yankees."

"What was your batting average?" I asked, happy to focus on baseball.

"Um," she said, looking at the ceiling as she sat down. "Three?"

"I don't think so," I said, joining her on the floor. "One or 1.000 or getting a hit 100 percent of the time is the best you can do in baseball, but it is basically impossible. Three is completely impossible."

There were now eight of us sitting on a furry rug on Andrea's basement floor. I recognized everyone except for one girl.

"Who's that?" I whispered to Thelma.

"That's Kamna," Thelma said. "She's one of my new best friends. I'll introduce you."

"No—" I don't know why, but I was feeling shy.

"Hey, Kamna," Thelma said. "This is Darcy. He plays baseball."

"Hello Darcy who plays baseball," she said coolly with a slight English accent.

"Um . . . hi," I said. She had black hair, cut to her shoulders, and dark brown eyes.

"All right, everyone," Andrea announced excitedly. "Time to get started!"

Andrea hopped up without a word and spun the bottle. It went around three times and stopped at Zoë Turnbull.

"Okay, Zoë. Now we need a boy!" Andrea said, clapping her hands together.

The bottle spun and eventually stopped at Marc Talbot. Zoë

made a face, and everyone giggled nervously. Andrea pointed them to a closet at the bottom of the stairs, and I started to feel a bit woozy.

The door had barely closed before Marc and Zoë came out again, one after the other.

"That was only six seconds," Andrea said, disappointed.

"We're timing the kisses?" I whispered to Thelma in a panic.

"I guess," she said, smiling.

If Thelma was nervous, she was doing a good job of hiding it. Andrea spun the bottle again, and it was soon pointing back at her. This time Andrea took a little longer to spin the bottle. All of the guys—including me—shifted nervously as she eyed us. She put one hand over her eyes, squealed, and then spun. The spout went around once quickly, and for a second I thought it was stopping at me, but it kept on going, pointing right at Greg Harwood. Andrea opened her eyes and smiled. Everyone oohed as Andrea and Greg disappeared behind the door.

It was silent in the room. Everyone looked back and forth between one another and the closet door. The seconds dragged by like minutes. Thelma put her hand to her mouth and started giggling. Finally, the door burst open, and Andrea and Greg stumbled out of the closet like smoke inhalation victims.

Zoë, who had been timing, said, "One minute and thirty-three seconds."

I swallowed. This was a serious game. And I knew that if I didn't do something soon I was going to be mouth-to-mouth with either Thelma or this new girl, Kamna.

I could hear Grandpa saying, "Looks like you're in a bit of a pickle, Darce."

Then suddenly, I was struck with a thought. Was this somehow going to ruin my chances with Danalda? It was *baseball* that was supposed to help me kiss a girl, not spin the bottle, and it was Danalda I was supposed to kiss. If she heard I had kissed somebody else, would it spoil everything?

I had to get out of Andrea's basement, but I didn't know how. I looked back at the stairs, my only means of escape.

"Here we go," Andrea said, spinning the bottle.

The bottle spun and stopped just to the left of Thelma.

"Thelma's a winner!" Andrea said, grabbing the bottle and giving it another big twirl. "Now who's the lucky guy going to be?"

The bottle spun four times and then began to slow. It finally stopped and was pointing right back at Thelma.

"It's closest to Darcy," Zoe said.

My stomach fell.

Andrea put her finger to her mouth. "I don't know. Franklin looks closer to me."

We both tried to shift.

"Look," Marc said. "Darcy's foot was, like, right beside her."

"It's where his whole body is that matters," Andrea said.

"We need a rulebook," Thelma said, giggling. "Just like in baseball, hey, Darce?"

I nodded at her, feeling a little sick. Didn't she understand what was happening? *We could be next.* I could barely breathe, let alone speak.

"Okay," Andrea said sternly. "Redo. But from now on everyone has to sit up and cross their legs, and it's whoever's closest. I'll get a tape measure if I have to."

Andrea spun the bottle impatiently, this time with little force. It spun once, and then it was definitely slowing toward me. It passed Thelma, and there was a voice from the stairwell.

"I'm coming down with some pop and chips," Mrs. Kraft announced. "Ready or not."

Andrea grabbed the bottle before it stopped.

My savior, Mrs. Kraft!

Andrea quickly hid the bottle under her couch and slid a movie into the machine. Everyone was silent as Mrs. Kraft put the food down on the table, except for me.

"Thanks," I said, getting up and grabbing a handful of chips. "This is really going to hit the spot."

"You're welcome, Darcy," Mrs. Kraft said. "And the rest of you, don't be shy."

I stood over the food and stuffed my face, and then I was *really* beginning to feel sick. At least I had an alibi. I walked over to Andrea with my hand on my stomach and told her I was sorry, but I wasn't feeling so hot and had to get home. Andrea started to protest, but I just turned and walked away. As I was going up the stairs, holding on tight to the railing, I looked over at Thelma, who was busy eating. Beside her was Kamna, who was glaring at me. I flew up the stairs.

I got my jacket and boots, thanked Mrs. Kraft, and escaped out the front door. By the time I got to the end of Andrea's driveway, I realized I'd forgotten to call home. I'd be home in minutes, anyway, I thought. As I walked past the mounds of street-lit snow, I felt bad about bailing on Thelma. After a while, I stopped on the sidewalk to look up at the few thick snowflakes falling from the darkened sky. I took a big breath of cold air, exhaled a cloud of condensation, and resumed my walk home.

As I neared our house, my mind began to clear. I had left the party for a good reason, I decided. Why? Because I was definitely going to get to first base with Danalda Chase and I was definitely going use my baseball knowledge and status to do it.

Winter ball had officially begun.

5

◆

NO MAN'S LAND

◆

in the hole **def.** When a batter is the next to step into the on-deck circle—i.e., not the next batter but the next-next batter up.

After the Christmas vacation, everything seemed new again. Ralph, Dwight, and I walked to school together on the first day. Dwight told us about the baseball video game he'd gotten for Christmas, and Ralph was sporting some new baggy pants that he thought would bring his "coolness to a whole new level." Neither Ralph nor Dwight was in my homeroom this year, but Thelma was. When I entered class that morning, she grabbed my arm and said, "Where did you disappear to the other night at Andrea's?"

"Um," I said feebly, "I had to go."

"Well, thanks," Thelma said sarcastically. "Kamna escaped right after you, and I was stuck kissing Franklin Lee."

"Sorry," I said. "Did you at least win the competition?"

Thelma shook her head and winced. "I don't think there's a watch that could time how short our kiss was."

At lunchtime, I found Ralph and Dwight in the back corner of the cafeteria, where they each had a big bowl of fries called the Gravy Mountain. They were sitting with Brett Neeson, who was from the Cool Crowd and was really more a friend of Ralph's. Brett was from Newton Primary, the school that Danalda had gone to. One of the weird things about going to junior high was that suddenly you were mixing with Newton students—"the enemy," as Dwight put it. Brett was in Ralph's English class and seemed like a nice enough guy, and he was just as girl-obsessed as Ralph. As soon as I sat down, Brett started talking about the upcoming Valentine's Day Dance.

"I'm going to ask Rachel Chow," Brett said.

"Yeah, I'm going to ask Simone tomorrow," Ralph said. "This is sooo going to rage."

"Rage? I'll show you rage!" Dwight shrieked. "You're not seriously thinking of going to that dance, are you, Ralph?"

"Of course I am!" Ralph snapped.

"Yeah," Brett said to Dwight. "Everyone's going to be there."

"Well, not me," Dwight said. "What about you, Darce?"

"Da-nal-da will be there," Ralph jumped in before I could answer.

"So?" I protested.

"Well," Ralph said, "you're going to ask her, aren't you?"

"Maybe," I said, looking away.

"Like I said before: you'd better act quickly," Ralph said, looking over at Brett, who nodded. "This isn't batting practice, you know."

"That's for sure," Dwight sneered. "Batting and dancing aren't even in the same ballpark."

"I don't know," I said to Dwight.

"That's my boy," Ralph said, patting me on the back and smiling at Brett.

My plan *was* to ask Danalda to the Valentine's Dance as soon as possible. My bat was definitely on my shoulder, and I felt like I was ready to hit. Danalda wasn't in any of my classes, so I was planning on catching her before class in the morning. The next day, I was chatting with Thelma, getting my books from my locker, when I saw Danalda talking to a friend. I figured this was my chance.

I told Thelma I'd see her in class just as Danalda began heading my way. Her long hair was loose over her shoulders, and she was wearing a pink sweater that all the girls seemed to be wearing. Danalda smiled when she saw me coming down the hall, which gave me a boost—at least she knew I existed. I decided not to wait to drop the question. I swallowed deeply and strode toward my fate. Danalda suddenly turned to a room on the right. I quickened my pace to see where she was going. I couldn't believe my eyes.

Danalda was talking to Vernon Maxwell in the doorway of Room 217. He was looking less confident than usual, shifting his bag on his shoulder and casting his eyes about nervously. That made *me* nervous. I watched him closely. He leaned down toward her and said something, and I would have bet my new glove that he was asking her to the Valentine's Day Dance.

Before Danalda turned, I slipped out of sight down the hallway. As I trudged toward class, I was feeling completely defeated. I was pretty sure Danalda was going to the dance with Vernon, and that meant my chances were finished. But then just as I got to class, another thought struck me: maybe I wasn't the leadoff hitter. Heck, I didn't even feel like I was on deck yet. It was a small consolation, but by the end of the day, I had it figured out: I was *in the hole.*

Being in the hole is one of the worst places to be. You are not sitting on the bench cheering on the team. You are not on the field concentrating on the play. You are not in the batter's box, trying to get a hit for your team. You are not even in the on-deck circle, drawing attention to your professional-looking swing. No one except maybe your grandfather is paying attention to you on the sidelines. But you are still in the game, trapped in no man's land, waiting for something to change.

The truth was I was "in the hole" in more ways than one.

Nap and Sam were almost as busy at the beginning of second term in January as they were at the end of first. Instead of being able to hang out after school with Ralph and Dwight or maybe have an opportunity to run into Danalda, I still had to go home every day right after the bell to look after Grandpa. It wasn't until mid-January that my parents finally had more free time and my responsibilities were pared down. Still, I had to come home every Tuesday and Thursday, when Nap was teaching and Sam had a yoga class.

At the end of the third week of January, Thelma came up to me at my locker.

"Hi, Darcy," she said cheerfully. "Do you want to go to the Valentine's Day Dance with me?"

"Um . . . well . . . I mean—"

"I know, I know," she said. "There was probably someone else you wanted to go with . . . but she's going with—"

"Excuse me?" I demanded.

"But," she said timidly, "she's going with Vernon?"

How did she know?

"Yeah, well. Maybe," I bobbled. "So . . ."

"So why don't *we* go?" she said. "Don't worry—we'll just go as friends, and it'll be fun." Then she leaned in and whispered, "You've got to help me. I heard Franklin is going to ask me this weekend."

I wasn't too happy about being used as a decoy, but it wasn't like I had a better plan.

"Okay," I said. "We'll go . . . *as friends.*"

"Great," she said, turning toward class. "I know a bunch of people we can go with."

That night at the dinner table, I realized I hadn't yet asked permission to go to the dance.

"Um," I said, not exactly knowing how to broach the topic. "I'm thinking of going to the Valentine's Day Dance."

"With who?" Beattie said. "Danalda?"

"None of your business," I snapped. Were all girls psychic?

"What about those grades of yours?" Nap said finally from the head of the table. "I don't know if they're good enough for you to go."

Earlier, I had made the mistake of leaving my books on the kitchen table, and Nap's eyes just so happened to pass through my science folder and see a so-so mark on a recent quiz.

"But that's so unfair," I complained, looking down at my plate.

There was silence.

"It *is* his first junior high dance, Dad," Sam finally said. Sam called Nap Dad, as a way of making up for us kids not doing it.

"Yeah, don't be such a gall-stoned stick-in-the-mud," Grandpa said with his fork raised at my dad.

"You stay out of this," Nap said, pointing a finger back at Grandpa. "A score of six out of ten on a science quiz is not good enough for this family."

There was silence at the table again. I was slowly eating my last piece of broccoli when Beattie stepped to the plate.

"Sheesh!" she yelled. "Let him go to the *gall-stoned* dance!"

There was a shocked silence and then another eruption of dispute. Between Grandpa's peals of laughter, Sam's "Don't you dare raise your voice like that, Beatrice!" and Nap's resounding "I've had enough out of you" across the table to Grandpa, I managed to excuse myself and clear off my plate. I decided to play my last card: a sad face and a tap on Sam's shoulder.

"What do you think?" I asked cautiously.

She looked over at Nap. "If you study hard this weekend, I can't see any reason why you shouldn't go to the dance!"

"Yes!" I said triumphantly.

I turned, winked at Beattie, and without giving Nap the opportunity to veto the decision, went upstairs to my room and cracked open my books.

6

◆

KEEPING YOUR HEAD
IN THE GAME

◆

on the ball **def.** There is a lot of inactive time in baseball, and it's easy to let your mind wander. When you are out in the field, on the bench, or in the hole, you should be on the ball, as in staying alert and paying attention to what is happening in the game.

Thelma seemed to be the social coordinator for her group of friends, the ones Ralph called the "In-Betweens." ("You know the type," Ralph said to me once. "Not exactly cool, but not geeky, either.") The Valentine's Day Dance was fast approaching. A week before, Thelma went all out, collecting money and actually ordering a limousine to pick the eight of us up at our various houses.

The night of the dance finally arrived, and I was the last pickup at seven-thirty. Despite my protest, the whole family—even Grandpa—came out to the front window to wave and watch me go. I'd told Thelma it was all right if she just waited in the limo, as it wasn't a real date. Still, she poked her head out the window and gave a big wave to my family. As I stepped onto our front stairs, I heard Grandpa say, "Knock 'em dead, Darcy!" I got into the limo and squeezed beside my date.

Thelma was actually kind of cute, but she felt more like a sister than anything. As soon as the limo started moving she introduced me to the In-Betweens I didn't know and tried to get me into the conversation. One of the girls was Kamna, the one who was at Andrea's party. She was still acting distant and cold, looking out the window instead of joining in. Her date, Alan, seemed to be nervous around her and kept joking around with the guy beside him.

When we got to the dance, I saw Ralph hanging out with the Cool Crowd in the corner of the dance floor. Simone had waited three weeks before accepting Ralph's invitation, and he was ready to burst when she finally did. Dwight stayed firm on his declaration that "dances are the stupidest things in the world," staying at home to play a baseball video game with his new friend, Liam. I was beginning to think that Dwight was right when Thelma suddenly disappeared with her friend Sara, who'd just been dumped by her boyfriend, and left me to fend for myself. I found a place to stand along one side of the dance floor, pretending to be interested as groups of girls and the occasional couple danced in front of me.

I looked around for Danalda and Vernon, but couldn't see them anywhere. My eyes returned to the dance floor when all of a sudden a couple emerged from behind a bunch of girls. It felt like someone had punched me in the stomach, and for a moment I couldn't breathe: it was them. Danalda was wearing a velvety dark green dress and Vernon's long arms around her back. The two of them were dancing close in slow circles, seeming to think that every song was a slow song! I didn't want to stare, but I couldn't help myself. After a couple of tunes, I tried to distract myself by looking for Ralph on the other side of the room. When I glanced back at the dance floor, Danalda and Vernon had disappeared.

I searched around and saw Kamna sitting alone at one of the round tables that surrounded the dance floor. I was feeling desperate to get off the I-lost-my-date loser-train, so I walked over.

"Hi there."

She looked up blankly.

"It's Darcy from the limo."

"And the spin-the-bottle party. I know, I remember," she said. "You aren't going to ask me to dance, are you?"

"No, no," I said. "I'm not really into dancing."

She stared at me intensely with her dark eyes.

"Really," she said. "What are you into?"

I looked down at my shoes. "Baseball."

"Oh, yeah, I remember," she said, looking away. "North American boys and their baseball."

"You don't like baseball?" I asked incredulously.

"What's there to like?"

"You've got to be kidding. Look . . . there's Randy Johnson, Babe Ruth, George Bre—"

"Stop," she said, covering her ears. "Look. My mom and dad are from England—India originally, if you hadn't noticed—and my dad made me sit through cricket games on the telly when I was a kid."

I went to protest, but her shooing hand stopped me.

"I know, I know," she droned. "I've heard it before. They are different sports. You wouldn't believe what my dad would do if he knew I was chatting with a baseball fan. But as far as I'm concerned, if there's a ball, a piece of wood used for hitting, and a heap of stupid statistics, I'm not interested."

I was stunned. And, somehow, hurt.

"Where's your date, what's his name, Alan?" I said meanly.

"He's dancing with the girl he wanted to go with," she said.

"Oh."

She really had a way of shutting you up.

"How about you? Where's your love gone to?" she said.

"Thelma's just a friend," I snapped back.

"No, I mean Danalda, the girl you've been looking for all night."

My face turned red, and I stood up quickly.

"Don't worry," she said. "Vernon will be history before the

end of the night. That's the way Danalda works. It's all about the Chase for Ms. Chase. She eats up boys for breakfast."

"You don't know what you're talking about," I said.

"Really?" she said, smirking.

"I'm going to see how Thelma is," I said.

Kamna just shrugged and looked off at the dance floor as I stomped out of the room, past the bathrooms, and outside.

The following Monday, Thelma came up to me before lunch.

"You want to have lunch in the caf with me?" she asked.

Lunch with Thelma meant lunch with the In-Between crowd. Did I want to become an In-Between? They weren't exactly baseball lovers, but at least they weren't caught up in the who's-cooler-than-who thing.

"Sure," I said finally. "Just let me put my books away."

Thelma came with me to my locker.

"So, the Valentine's Dance was more like a breakup dance, huh, Darce?" Thelma said.

"What do you mean?"

"Well," she said. "Along with Sara and Todd breaking up, I heard Danalda dumped Vernon and Simone dumped Ralph."

"Really?" I said, trying not to sound hopeful about Danalda.

"So maybe you have a chance with her after all," she suggested gently.

"Whatever," I said, turning and walking away so that she couldn't see my burning face.

"Hey, wait up, will you?"

Thelma caught up with me, and when we got to the cafeteria there were only two seats left at the In-Betweens' usual table by the windows. Thelma quickly took a seat beside a couple of guys, and I was stuck on the end near two girls. Across from me was Kamna.

"Mr. Baseball. Welcome to the window seat," Kamna said, blinking her black eyes at me. "Is this a step up or have you been demoted from a cooler crowd?"

"Umm . . . I'm . . . I'm just here for–"

"The gray beef burgers and the soggy fish and chips?"

I tried to get my wits about me. "I've always been more partial to the Gravy Mountain," I stated.

"A very good choice. A truly tasty delight. You know, I think you're really going to fit in around here."

The girl beside me shook her head and ate her sandwich as if this was Kamna's usual way. I started to get up for the said fries—and a little break from Kamna's interrogation—when she started in again.

"Tell me," she said, leaning on her elbow and smiling, "what does a baseball-crazy guy do for all these horrible winter months?"

"What do you care? I thought you hated baseball."

"Well, I do," she said matter-of-factly. "But I know how my father feels during the cricket off-season, and the pain on his face . . . I don't know . . . it *does* put me in a pretty good mood, but it also completely amazes me. How can a grown man be so attached to such a stupid game?"

I was no cricket player, but I felt it was my duty to defend the true wonder of being a sports fan. The problem was my mind and mouth couldn't agree on how my argument would begin.

"But—the problem—well, you see . . . if you just—"

"A very convincing position, Darcy, but I am having a bit of a problem with the beginning part."

The girl beside me giggled into her hand, and I could feel my face burning. I waited for a moment to collect myself. It seemed Kamna's attitude at the dance was not an exception.

I finally forced out a sentence. "I'm going to get some—"

"Let me guess," she called out like in a pop quiz. "Fries!"

I pushed my chair away and looked down the table at Thelma, who was happy in conversation.

"You see?" Kamna said as I stormed off. "I'm already getting to know you better."

I went up to the cafeteria line, trying to shake off my interaction with Kamna. I had to focus on Danalda. Now that she was available, I was going to get my chance. I didn't feel like I was in the hole anymore, still practicing my swings, but I also felt pretty far away from on deck. Maybe I was wrong about the beginning of my game. Maybe, I thought, my team took the field first.

7

◆

TAKING
THE FIELD

◆

running bases **def.** A game in which a player runs to and fro
between two bases, scoring a run each time he gets a new
bag, while two basemen try to throw him/her out. After an
out, the three players rotate.

The spring arrived early and so did the Cheetahs Baseball Team
sign-up sheet. I had been checking for the list since the beginning of March, and on the third Thursday of the month, it
finally went up. I was the first to put my name down. I stepped
back and stared at the sheet that I knew would fill up with the
best players in Cherrydale. I was hoping Danalda would at least
notice that my name was at the top, that I was a real ballplayer.
As I walked away and down the hall, I felt like I had taken a big

step: winter ball was now officially over, spring training for the real season had finally begun, and I was ready to take the field.

Dwight called just as I got home from school that afternoon.

"Darcy!" he shrieked as soon as I'd answered the phone. "I signed up right below you! I can't believe it's finally here!"

"Me, too. I'm totally pumped," I said.

"I called Ralphy-boy," Dwight continued, sounding like he was still in primary school. "I convinced him to meet at the park to throw the ball around."

"Really?"

"Yeah. He said, 'Call Darcy. And don't bring that Liam friend of yours, or I'll tell him you still wet your bed.'"

I laughed and then paused. "Wait a sec. I think there's something I'm supposed to do this aft."

"What? Are you crazy?" Dwight asked. "And miss finally throwing the ball around? What could be more important?"

"Okay, okay," I said, swept up in the excitement. "I'll see you there in ten."

I rushed upstairs and got my new glove and ball from under my bed. I grabbed an apple and my spring jacket. Without another thought, I flew out the door.

There's nothing quite like the excitement of the first throws of spring. The hard ball feels heavier than you remember and maybe even a little small. It's usually cold outside, so when the ball hits your glove there's a real snap when you catch it right.

When you don't, when the ball hits your palm instead of the mitt, a cold shock of pain goes up your arm. When Ralph laughs at your wincing face and Dwight tells you to hurry up and throw the ball, you know that spring has finally come and that the baseball season has officially begun.

It was sunny, but there was still a little bite in the air. There were still a few patches of snow where there used to be big piles. I found Dwight already at the park, tossing a ball up in the air and talking to himself. If left alone with a ball and glove, Dwight was apt to entertain himself with play-by-play. As I approached, I heard something like "He's got a track on the ball, he gets under it, he—"

"Hey, Dwight!" I yelled.

Dwight jerked, surprised, and the ball landed on the ground beside him. "—and he misses it because his friend Darcy likes to see his friends eat baseballs."

"No, no, Dwight," I said as he bent down for the ball. "Not all of my friends . . . just you."

"Funny," he said, throwing it at me hard.

I snagged the ball out of the air.

"Nice glove," he said.

"Thanks," I said, bending it over the ball. "I've been trying to work it in, but it's going to take a while. Hey, where's Ralph?"

"Fashionably late, of course. Too-cool Ralphy-boy can arrive anytime he wants."

I threw the ball back lightly.

"How's things?" I said.

"Not bad, not bad," he said. "I finally took Liam down in our video baseball match in extra innings the other night and he hasn't talked to me since. I'll wait a couple more days before I start rubbing it in. How 'bout you? How's the In-Between crowd?"

"Not bad."

"Kamna is in my homeroom," Dwight said. "Man, is she cold!"

"You're not kidding."

There was a holler off in the distance. We both turned to see Ralph walking through the gates of the park, waving his glove in the air. He was calling for one of us to throw the ball. Dwight held it in his glove.

"You're too far off," he said in a normal voice as if Ralph were right there. He grabbed the ball with his bare hand and looked over at me. "He's too far off."

I shrugged my shoulders.

"You're too far off," he finally said loudly enough.

"Oh, yeah," Ralph said as he ran up. "I forgot about your arm. Weak and inaccurate."

Dwight held on to the ball until Ralph was standing in front of us.

"Surprised you could make it out for once," Dwight quipped. "I guess baseball is cool again."

"What can I tell ya?" Ralph said, snapping his fist into his glove. "It smells like baseball today. Now, how about that ball?"

Ralph put his glove out, but Dwight shook his head. "Step back," he said, "and I'll show you heat that'll remind you of black tar in the summer."

Ralph laughed, but with less edge, and slapped me on the back with his glove. "We'll toss it around a bit, then play a little running bases. Darcy's the runner."

That couple of hours, the three of us were transported. No girls, cool clothing, worried parents, or homework could come between us. Ralph and Dwight were laughing as I ran back and forth, the ball arcing over my head, forcing me this way and that. By the time I was put out with thirteen runs under my belt, my knees were brown with spring mud and my jacket, used as one of the bases, was a canvas of footprints.

After each of us played runner, we were tired. We dropped to the ground, even though it was cold and wet, and the sky was getting dark.

"That was wicked!" Ralph said, looking up to the sky, breathing heavily, leaning on an elbow. "We should play more often."

Dwight and I were silent. It was Ralph who was never around.

"Well, you've got the Cheetah tryouts," Dwight said coolly.

"Nah, actually, I know this is going to sound crazy, but I didn't sign up. I don't think I'm going to try out."

"What're you talking about?" Dwight said. "We've been waiting for this all our lives. And you just said we should play more often!"

"With the three of us, it's different," Ralph said nicely. "I dunno . . . I'm not going to make the team, anyway."

It wasn't true. Ralph was a natural, and he had the best chance out of the three of us.

". . . and," he continued, "I think I'm going to audition for the school play."

"The play?" Dwight exclaimed. "I don't believe it! You're crazy! I can't believe you'd just quit baseball."

"And there's other stuff as well," Ralph said to his feet.

"Oh, right . . . other stuff," Dwight said sourly. "What about you, Darce? You giving up to?"

"Nah, I'll give it a go. Might as well try, right?"

"Hey, man," Ralph jumped in. "You gotta do what you gotta do."

Dwight snorted, and I looked away.

"It's getting cold," Ralph said. "I've got to split this banana."

As Ralph walked away, I turned and saw that he had mud all over his pants, grass sticking out like hay from a scarecrow.

"Nice butt," I said.

"Yeah," he said, turning his head back with a smile. "Nice face."

Dwight didn't look up as Ralph walked away. He just pulled at the leather straps of his glove.

"Nice life," he finally said as if Ralph were still beside him.

When I got home, I threw my glove on the living room sofa and went back to the kitchen. Nap was on the phone, Sam had her back to me at the kitchen table, and Beattie was pretending to get down to her homework. She did a quick throat-slit, you're-in-big-trouble sign at me as Sam turned around.

"Darcy Jonathan Spillman, where have you been?" Sam demanded. It was Nap who usually used my three names threateningly. I did not recognize Sam's tone as she quickly stood up from her kitchen seat.

"I was just throwing—"

"Did I not remind you this morning about coming home at four o'clock to take care of your grandfather?"

"But," I protested, "no one was here when I came home, and Dwight called about the sign-up sheet—"

"What sign-up sheet?"

"For the Cheetahs."

"Darcy, can we forget about baseball for once . . . *please?*"

I glared at my mom. I was just about to snap at her when Nap finally spoke into the phone. He'd been standing, staring at Beattie's fridge art with the phone to his ear. Suddenly, he spoke in an official-sounding voice. His body was tense, moving in jerks as he spoke.

"Yes, I'd like to report a missing person. That's right. Joseph Spillman. He's eighty-three."

8

♦

CALLING FOR THE BALL

♦

to wave a player off **def.** When two fielders are headed for
the same hit ball (usually a pop-up), one or the other, usually
the one in the best position, takes command, says, "I got it!"
and waves his hand to tell the other player to move away.

I stood there, muddy and cold, as Beattie still pretended to study
at the table. Her face was deep in her textbook, but her eyes were
leveled across at me.

"You should have been here. It was your responsibility," Sam
said in an angry whisper as Nap spoke with the police.

My face reddened. I wanted to scream at her for suggesting
that I'd purposely forgotten about taking care of Grandpa. But
the fact of the matter was, I was mad at myself, too, because

it was me who called for the ball. *Sure, Sam. No problemo. I'll remember.* And when you call for the ball, wave someone off, and then the ball hits the ground like a bomb, there's only one person responsible. I flew up to my room, trying to hold back tears.

Ten minutes later, Sam was at my door.

"Darcy, you in here?" Sam's voice was softer, and she gave her three respectful knocks before coming in.

I was lying on my bed, the mud on my pants starting to dry and flake off onto the blankets.

"Darcy, you should take those muddy clothes off."

I didn't answer.

She sighed. "We found Grandpa. The police called back to say that there was an old man at Zak's Donuts raising hell about coconut donuts."

A small smile broke across my face as I turned toward her. Grandpa was always giving Zak trouble about taking Coconut Dreams off his menu a couple of years ago ("I've been eating them *gall-stoned* coconut buggers since 1951!" he'd say).

"Yeah," she said with a little laugh. "I guess we can always count on Grandpa being noticed. Nap's gone to get him."

"Oh," I said, turning my head back toward the wall, the rush of my earlier anger shooting through me.

"Hey," Sam said, sitting on the end of my bed, putting her hand on my foot and giving it a little shake. "Sorry about yelling at you like that. It wasn't all your fault."

"Yeah, it was," I said, pressing my cheek farther into the bed. "I called for the ball."

"What?" she asked.

Beattie called for her from downstairs.

"Nothing," I said. "Just stupid baseball stuff."

Sam got up. "Darcy . . . I didn't mean to say that about baseball."

She stood over me silently for a moment, then went to see what Beattie wanted.

Two days later, on Saturday, while Grandpa and Sam were at the doctor (Grandpa wouldn't go with Nap), we had a "partial" family meeting. Nap was sitting in his usual seat at the head of the kitchen table, and Beattie was in her seat to his right. I sat in Grandpa's chair across the length of the table, my arms crossed and my bottom lip bitten. Bullets of rain exploded against the kitchen window.

Nap sighed before he spoke. "Grandpa is sick, and your mother and I . . . we . . . the family, don't have enough . . . resources . . . to take care of him."

I clucked my tongue angrily and watched the bullets turn to water and stream angrily down the window.

"It's no one's fault," he said defensively. "Grandpa is having trouble and he needs to be watched . . . cared for . . . all the time."

There were raindrops and silence.

"Your mother and I have been trying to get our schedules

in sync, but it's just too difficult. We are both teaching spring courses at different campuses. Darcy, your life is more complicated now with junior high; it's not fair to put these demands on you. Beattie, you need to focus on your schoolwork."

To this, Beattie threw her elbows on the table and put her chin in her hands.

I could feel pressure on my head, and my throat began to tighten. The rain was falling hard, and I could not take my eyes away from the window.

"We . . . I . . . your mother and I just wanted to tell you," Nap said. "We have found a retirement home for Grandpa. A place where he'll be safe . . . and happy. They can take him next Saturday. The waiting lists are long at most places." He paused. "I know this is sudden. Darcy . . . Beattie?"

I snorted and kicked the bottom of the table leg.

"Guys?"

"I'm not a guy, Dad!" Beattie said. She seemed confused by what was happening, but she could tell that I was angry and wanted to be on my side.

"Darcy?"

"What does Grandpa want?" I said, still looking away.

"Darcy, you know your grandfather. He's not going to jus—"

"Fine with me, then," I interrupted. I turned and looked at him, unfocused. "Can I go now?"

"Yeah, me too," Beattie droned. She was holding her head with her thumbs, looping them under her ears.

Nap leaned forward, ready to speak, but something stopped him. He froze, then fell back in his seat. "Sure," he said. "You can go."

Ralph called to chat that night. He'd been doing this occasionally since February, when he stopped coming to our table at the cafeteria because he didn't get along with Dwight's new friend, Liam. Anyway, he seemed kind of lonely.

"Darce-man. Whatcha doing tonight?"

"Oh . . . I don't know. Staying home, I guess."

"I got the lines for the school play," he said. "It's *Dracula*. I'm trying out for this character, Renfield, who eats flies and talks to himself."

"Sounds perfect."

"Funny," he said dryly. "Hey, you've been hanging out with the In-Betweens a lot lately."

"So?"

"Hey," Ralph said, distracted. "I've got something to tell you."

"What?"

"I heard that Danalda rated you the third-cutest guy in seventh grade, behind Jim Charleston and Greg Harwood."

"You're kidding." I couldn't believe my ears.

"I don't kid about girls," Ralph said. "So when are you gonna make your move?"

"Soon," I said. "Remember what you said about girls and baseball in the fall?"

"What are you talking about, 'girls and baseball'?"

"You know—about 'getting to first base,'" I blurted out. "And how the Cheetah tryouts were our last chance."

"I didn't say that. You're whacked, Darce-man. Completely gonzo."

"Listen," I snapped. "I've come up with a plan: baseball is going to help me get to first base with Danalda."

"Really, Darce," Ralph said. "Maybe you *should* go see a doctor!"

"Listen," I repeated. "Even Grandpa Spillman said that baseball and love had something—"

"Your grandpa?" Ralph laughed. "If there's anyone more whacked than you, it's Grandpa Spillman."

"Shut up, Ralph." I tried to keep my voice calm.

"What?" he said casually. "You know as well as I do that your grandpa is a couple of players short of a full lineup."

"Shut your mouth." I was now yelling in a whisper, my head leaning against the wall.

Deep down, I knew he was just kidding, but I couldn't help reacting. "So, how's Simone these days, Ralph-man? I heard she dumped you."

"Well, it's not exactly how it happened."

"Yeah, well, that's what I heard."

"Darce-man, look. I can't be a superstud all the—"

I hung up.

I'd never hung up on anyone in my life. I just couldn't listen to him anymore. I stormed toward my room, passing Beattie, who was alarmingly close to where I'd been standing.

"Darcy?" she said.

"Yeah."

I should have heard the return of her little-sister voice.

"If you think kissing girls and baseball have anything to do with each other, you are nutso!"

"Beattie," I said calmly. "Out!!!!"

I lay fuming on my bed for an hour. But before I finally turned off my light, I made three clear decisions:

1. I was done with fielding.
2. My game with Danalda was going to start in the batter's box.
3. I needed to get some *real* practice swings in, because I was only one small step away from the real deal.

9

PRACTICE SWINGS

on deck **def.** When a player is the next to go into the batter's box to face the pitcher, he is on deck.

On Monday morning, I was going to English class when Kamna caught me by the arm.

"Hey, how're ya doing?"

"Not bad," I said suspiciously.

"I hear you're trying out for the Cheetahs this year."

"What would you know about the Cheetahs? You hate baseball."

"Yeah," she said, trying to hold something back. "But I also hear you've got a theory."

"What do you mean?"

"Well, Ralph is in my social studies class, and he just started talking to me at the end of class yesterday. He mentioned something about your theory about girls and baseball."

My face burned. *Blabbermouth Ralph,* I thought. What was he doing telling Kamna this?

"Oh, yeah . . . so what?" I said, trying to keep it together.

"Well, I know this might sound strange, but I've been thinking that maybe I could give you a hand."

Her face was straight and serious.

"Listen," I told her. "I don't know what you and Ralph are up to, but—"

"No, no," she said, waving her hands in front of her. "I don't even really know the guy. I mean, I was just thinking . . . I could help you. "

"I don't want any help!"

"Maybe that's your first mistake," she said bluntly.

"Maybe you're nuts," I said, turning away toward my classroom.

"Maybe," I heard her say as I stormed away.

Beattie found me sitting by myself in the kitchen after school. The house was empty, as Nap, Sam, and Grandpa were visiting the retirement home together.

"Whatcha doing?" she said.

"Nothin'," I said glumly.

"Shouldn't you be getting ready for your tryouts?"

"Maybe, but Ralph and I aren't speaking, and Dwight is always hanging out with this guy Liam—"

"Darcy," she said, making her voice like Grandpa's. "That's not the Spillman attitude. I'll get the bat and ball. You grab your glove and meet me in the backyard. And we'll see what we can do about that fielding of yours."

Beattie helped me with fielding practice until late in the evening. She hit me short grounders until I got ten in a row. It took a while, because I was still trying to work in my new glove. In return, I agreed to help her with her math homework, which amounted to Beattie reading the questions and me doing all the work.

As for batting practice, I was still sort of stuck. Beattie didn't have the strongest arm, and we would have to go to the diamond for more space. I did not want to be seen taking pitches from a munchkin, even a superstar munchkin. Junior high pitchers were going to be that much better at throwing a fastball and a curve, and a few might even have a third pitch. With or without preseason batting practice, hitting a Cheetah pitch was going to be tough.

When I opened my locker on Tuesday morning, a folded-up piece of paper fell to the floor. I picked up the letter and read it.

Getting the Girl Rule #1:

GET TO KNOW, BE FRIENDLY WITH, FLATTER, BE HELPFUL TO, TRY TO SPEAK AS MUCH WITH THE GIRL'S BEST FRIEND.

A GIRL WILL ALWAYS ASK HER BEST FRIEND WHAT SHE THINKS OF A GUY BEFORE SHE DECIDES HE'S WORTH GOING FOR. (FOR MORE INFORMATION JUST CALL—I'M IN THE SCHOOL DIRECTORY.)

From the time that I finished the letter until the moment I grabbed our home phone later in the afternoon, it was all I could think about. I was furious.

A woman with a thick East Indian accent answered. "Yes?"

"Hello, is Kamna there, please?"

"Yes, Kamna is here. Who is calling?"

"It's Darcy . . . Darcy Spillman . . . I'm a frie—I mean, I know Kamna from school."

"What is this about?"

I wasn't exactly prepared for the third degree.

"Umm . . . Kamna is helping me with . . . umm . . . a project."

"Okay," the voice said skeptically as the receiver fell with a clonk. The woman's voice called out, followed shortly by two muffled voices yelling back and forth for at least a minute. There was silence, and then I heard the receiver dragged along slowly.

"Hello." It was Kamna.

"Hi. It's Darcy. What's the big idea with all this Getting the Girl crap?"

"Oh, sure, sure," she said, not answering. "No problem, just let me get my textbook."

"Kamn—"

The phone clonked down again, and I sat waiting for another minute.

"Hello, Darcy. I've got it. What did you need to know?"

"Listen," I said, trying to get my fire back, "what you need to know is I don't need any of your help!"

"Sorry about my mom," Kamna whispered softly. "She's a little strict about the phone."

"No problem," I said, frustrated that my point was not getting across. "What's the deal with this Rule Number One stuff?"

"Well," she said, still half whispering, "if you get on the good side of the best friend, you'll at least get a date or something."

"No, I mean . . . forget it . . . I don't need your help, okay?"

"Listen," she said, still whispering. "If you want to strike out, that is your own prerogative, as my dad would say, but you know, you don't seem like the kind of player who ignores a tip from the . . . what's it called . . . swinging coach."

"It's the hitting or batting coach," I corrected her. "And who says I'm going to strike out?"

"Sure—I mean, I guess anyone can get a hit every once in a while. Right?"

"Yeah, but . . . Listen . . . Just no more advice, okay?"

"Okay," she said, laughing. "But remember to keep your eye on the ba—"

I hung up. I went downstairs and told Beattie that I was ready for some grounders. She was watching TV and didn't want to budge. I turned the TV off and stood in front of it. She got up, silent and sour, knowing better than to argue. Beattie didn't say a word on her way down the deck stairs—she just went to her place at the end of the backyard and started swinging, giving me hard one-hoppers at my feet. I missed or bobbled almost every ball, even the softer ones she gave me later on. I finally got three in a row, and Beattie dropped the bat.

"That's it. I'm done," she said, walking away. "You're never going to make the Cheetahs if you field like that."

I was about to snap back at her, but she was right. Everything about me felt awkward and out of control. Suddenly I had hung up on two people, when I'd never done it before in my life. I'd basically lost my two best friends. I'd gotten my grandpa sent to virtual prison, and I couldn't field a grounder for the life of me.

I couldn't get to sleep when I went to bed that night. I tossed and turned, thinking about what Kamna had said on the phone. I argued with her in my head, telling her again and again to mind her own business. Still, when I got to school the next day, I couldn't help paying more attention to Jennifer Crumble, Danalda's best friend. It just so happened that Jennifer was in three of my classes, and I found myself slowing down to say hi to her as we entered class, or passing her desk on my way out. With an amazing stroke of fate, two days after my note from Kamna, Jennifer and I had ended up in the same lab group for science, which meant unscience-like gabbing all class long. Jennifer was one of those cool girls who'd never said a word to me in sixth grade, but because the other two members of our group were from Newton Primary, Jennifer was friendlier than usual.

Whenever Mr. Lyon came by to check how our experiment was going, Jennifer had an amazing way of sounding like we were very interested in the experiment but were just having trouble getting started. In these lab talks, we became friends, or at least "class friends," which was almost as good.

The next day, I was grabbing a book from my locker between periods when Jennifer, Simone, and Danalda walked by, and Jennifer waved.

"Hi there, lab partner!" she said.

I smiled, and all three of them, including Danalda, smiled back. I was ready to step up to the plate.

10

◆

GETTING TOSSED FROM THE GAME

◆

the thumb **def.** A term describing the thumbing action an umpire uses when he throws someone out of a game.

On Thursday night, it finally sank in that Grandpa was moving out. I was upstairs doing homework on my bed after dinner when I heard Nap and Grandpa arguing. They were trying to pare down Grandpa's stuff—he was going to have much less room at the Home—and they couldn't agree on what should go with him, what should stay with us, and what should go in the trash.

I heard Nap yell, "When are you *ever* going to use this again?"

"What do you care?" Grandpa demanded. "Don't be so *gall-stoned* selfish!"

"Listen, Dad," Nap snapped, "I'm not being selfish. We have only so much space in the basement."

"I can't believe this!" Grandpa roared. "You're moving me into a teeny-weeny cell, and *you're* complaining about space."

I didn't want to hear it. I got up to shut the door, but I stopped when I heard the murmur of Sam's soothing voice. I stood there, listening to her calm them both down. She was amazing that way. After a minute or two, things were quiet again. I tried to get back to my homework, but it was hard. I couldn't believe Grandpa was really going away.

I wanted to talk to Grandpa. I got up to go downstairs, but then I heard Nap's heavy footfalls on the stairs. I was sure that he'd head straight for his office, so I decided to wait until he had settled in. He thumped past my door, creaked into his office, and *slammed* his door.

"Maybe . . . not," I whispered to myself, flopping back onto my bed.

The next afternoon I rushed home from school to see Grandpa, but he wasn't in his favorite chair, nor was he in the living room. I checked his room—it was almost completely empty.

I found Sam in the kitchen, flipping through a magazine.

"Where's Grandpa?"

"He's gone to the Home," Sam said plainly. "Didn't Nap tell you last night?"

"No," I said. "Not after all that yelling. When he finally came upstairs, he just went to his office and slammed the door."

"Oh, right. I think I heard that," Sam said, grimacing. "Darcy, I know this is hard. For everyone. Change is always difficult, especially such a big one as this."

"You're not kidding," I said, turning to go to my room.

"Darcy," Sam called out.

"Yeah," I said.

"We're going to visit him tomorrow. 'Kay?"

"Fine with me," I said, and went up to my room.

The next day, the whole family did go to visit Grandpa. It was a disaster. Somehow Nap had gotten his times mixed up, and we arrived right after Grandpa's nap. This was not smart. It always took Grandpa a good hour before he was even close to conversational. Before all of us could cram into his room at the Home, which *was* as small as a jail cell, Nap and Grandpa had started arguing about where everyone would sit. Then Grandpa suddenly got very grumpy, and Sam decided it was time for us to go.

The next morning, I decided to go see Grandpa on my own. I woke up at about eight-thirty, had a quick bowl of cereal, and managed to escape the house without an interrogation. I knew that I could catch the 5A bus to get myself to the Home. I packed a knapsack as well, with an apple and the autobiography of former Kansas City Royal Hall of Fame third baseman George Brett.

When I arrived at the Home, I was feeling nervous about seeing Grandpa on my own. Marion, the woman at the front desk, looked at the log in front of her and said that he had just finished his meal and was most likely in his room. I slunk down the hallway, trailing my hand along the wall, catching air on door frames until I reached Room 112. I knocked like Sam, three times softly.

There was no answer.

I gave it three more knocks, but harder.

"Go away! I'm not in the buying mood today. Take your sets of knives somewhere else."

This is what Grandpa always said when someone came knocking at the front door.

"It's me, Grandpa. Darcy!" I said, laughing.

"Darcy Spillman?" I heard him say, his voice getting closer. "You mean, the all-star third baseman for the Cherrydale Cheetahs? It can't be."

The door swung open to Grandpa's face. He was wearing his favorite red-and-green-plaid shirt with a plain white shirt underneath. Even when he was joking, he didn't break a smile.

"I don't know about all-star third baseman for any team, Grandpa," I said, no longer nervous.

"Darcy, you are—"

"I know, I know, Grandpa," I said as I walked in. "You are what you think you are."

"Yer gall-stoned right," Grandpa said.

I asked Grandpa how it was in the Home. He just mumbled and waved his hand at me like he didn't want to talk about it. I told him about school for a while, but it wasn't until I brought up baseball that his face lit up and he actually started listening.

"Beattie's helping me with my fielding in the backyard," I informed him.

"What about your pals?" he demanded.

"Dwight and Ralph? They're kind of not around as much."

"I'd give them a good whopping if they were mine."

"And," I said carefully, "I'm also sort of trying to ask this girl on a date. I'm treating it like an at-bat so I can, like, 'get to first base.' I'm on deck, and now that tryouts are starting soon, I'll step to the plate and she'll see that I'm a real ballplayer and—"

Grandpa was looking confused. *Maybe he's forgotten our conversation about baseball and love,* I thought. His eyes were shifting around, and his hand began tapping the arm of the chair. His eyebrows came together, and the lines on his forehead became a stack of wavy creases. After a long pause, he spoke.

"Your mother," he said, looking over in my direction, but not at me. "She was beautiful . . . but she was too darned soft on you."

"You mean Sam?" I said, confused.

He looked back out the window. "She said, 'Don't be so hard on him. He's just a boy.'"

His mouthed tightened.

"Sure," he said angrily. "You were young. What did I say when you were this high?" He put his hand three feet above the ground as his voice got louder. 'Get the ball back into the infield,' is what I said. How many times? But you just held on to it. That big kid, Norman Duffy, he was running, but you just held on. I was screaming from the bleachers and everyone was looking up at me. 'Throw the ball, Nap!' I said. 'Throw the *gall-stoned* ball!'"

He was yelling now with his fist up above his head, his left arm bracing him, trembling.

I was terrified. "Um, what are you talking about, Grandpa?"

"Don't you give me that, you little—"

Someone knocked on the door and came in. It was a nurse. At the sight of her, Grandpa froze, and then he began to cry. He burrowed his head in his hands, shaking.

"What did you say to him?" she said to me. I shook my head, and no words came out.

"It's okay, Mr. Spillman," she said, pointing me in the direction of the door. "It's okay. Visiting time is over. Time to quiet down."

I stepped into the corridor and ran.

I tore across the front lawn and across the street. I passed the bus stop and kept on running for several blocks. I stopped when I ran out of breath. I put my hands on my knees, and my chest was heaving. I closed my eyes. I waited. My breath slowed. I opened my eyes and began walking slowly to the next bus stop.

On the bus, I opened a window wide. The breeze cooled my face and whipped through my hair. The wind tickled my eyes, unlocking light tears that were pushed across my face like rain on a car window. I didn't wipe them off, and when I stopped crying, I could feel streaks of dry trails across my tight face.

Grandpa blamed me for everything that was happening, for his being put in the Home, for his forgetting about Grandma, baseball, and love, and for whatever had happened in a game I never played in.

11

◆

GOING OUT
FOR THE TEAM

◆

taking grounders **def.** A term used to describe infield practice.

The first day of tryouts was Monday, and I was ready to step in the batter's box. Unfortunately, Coach Rizzuto had other plans. We were asked to sit down by the backstop.

"Good . . . afternoon, boys, and welcome to the Cherrydale . . . Cheetahs Baseball Tryouts," he yelled out from the mound.

Coach Rizzuto spoke slowly and always looked slightly above your head. He also paused and winced in the strangest places. He had a big red nose and wore a faded yellow-and-black cap that someone said was his first-ever Cheetah hat from twenty years ago.

"Does anyone . . . know my winning percentage to this day?" he asked.

Several hands, including Dwight's, went up. There were a handful of second-year players who would have known this, but Coach Rizzuto wasn't looking for an answer from the crowd.

"It's .883," he said. "That's right. Point eight . . . eight . . . three."

We all sat silently against the backstop.

"Does anyone know why . . . I'm telling you this?"

Fewer hands went up this time.

"I'm telling you . . . this because I want my winning percentage to get better this year."

I looked over at Dwight, who was staring at Coach Rizzuto in awe.

"All right, boys. Let's . . . play some baseball."

Coach Rizzuto told the players to get into three groups: infielders, outfielders, and pitchers/catchers. I went with the infielders and Dwight went with the outfielders. He had played some shortstop in Little League, but there were three guys better than him at that position. My chances were probably greater making outfield, but Grandpa and I had decided: I was a third baseman through and through: no pretending I was something—someone—else. Sherman Smith was the first to take the third-base position, and I was next in line. Sherman was a shoo-in starter for the team. There was no other second-year third baseman to compete with, and Sherman had a great glove, a great arm, and a great bat. I knew my only chance to make the team was as the backup third baseman or as a utility player, someone who could play several positions.

Sherman took some easy grounders from Coach Rizzuto (his assistant coaches, Chuckie and Mr. Hart, were leading the outfielders and pitchers), who nodded, impressed, and then switched him off. I made sure my socks were pulled up high like Grandpa's and stepped onto the field. As I was passing Sherman outside the dugout, he said, "If you make this team, Spillman, I'll eat my jockstrap."

Along with being the one of the best ballplayers in the area, Sherman Smith was about the biggest jerk you ever met.

I settled into my position and readied myself for the oncoming grounders. The first grounder is always the most intense—it seems to either bolster or absolutely kill your confidence.

Coach Rizzuto pointed his bat at me and said, "Ready, Spillman? To first."

I nodded hard, pulling my hat down.

Coach Rizzuto threw the ball up and whacked a good hard one right at me.

You never know what a ball is going to do once it hits the ground. Sometimes it will bounce up high and soft, and other times it will shoot low between your legs. The first hit that Coach Rizzuto smacked at me was neither. It was a perfectly easy ball to field, hard but with a regular bounce right to my waist. The ball snapped into my glove, and it jerked a little from the force. I picked the ball from my glove while stutter-stepping toward first and threw an easy, accurate toss.

"Nice one, Spillman," Coach Rizzuto said. "A little more . . . zip on the ball next time."

I nodded back at him and stayed in position while he hit around the rest of the infield. My nerves were now steady, and I was ready to play my favorite game in the world.

The first tryout ended up being only a fielding one. Coach Rizzuto said if you couldn't field, you were never going to find yourself in the batter's box. I only fumbled one ball all afternoon, but Coach Rizzuto wasn't exactly giving us the toughest grounders. Dwight and a few outfielders were kept behind for more pop-ups, so I headed toward home. As I was walking away from the diamond, I ran into Kamna.

"Nice socks, Mr. Baseball," Kamna said, giggling.

"What are you doing here?" I asked, irritated.

"Last time I checked it was a free country," she said, smiling. "But if you must know, Thelma and I were watching the tryouts on top of the hill. She had to go home early. Great catching, by the way!"

"You mean fielding. Um . . . thanks . . . yeah," I said shyly, beginning to walk toward home. "I've got to keep that up if I'm going to make the team."

"You know you can't sound that way around Danalda," Kamna said, trailing along beside me. "Girls like her don't go for um-I'm-not-sure kind of guys! You've got to be spot-on, ace of the team, at least in your mind, or you'll never have a chance." She paused. "I noticed you are following Rule Number One. Looks like you made a new friend." She gave a cheesy thumbs-up sign.

"Look," I said as we walked along. "What's the deal? What do you care about me and Danalda?"

She looked away, thinking.

"Um . . . I don't know," she said finally. "You're going to think I'm crazy, but ever since we came here from London three years ago—we lived there for a couple of years in between here and India—I've always felt sort of different. You know, out of it. Indian culture is totally different, very English, more strict and proper. That's how I was brought up. I just think an Indian boy would never come up with the baseball/love thing, or whatever, cricket and love."

She laughed. "I remember hearing 'getting to first base' at Newton, and apart from the fact that my parents would kill me if I so much as mentioned the word 'boy,' I was confused about why kissing was called 'getting to first base.' I finally asked someone, but I still didn't really understand. What's the connection? Then, when Ralph told me about your idea, whatever his reasons were, I didn't think it was crazy of you, because it's like, right there. Getting to first base . . . I actually thought it was sort of smart. So here's the crazy part: I was thinking that maybe if I learned some stuff about baseball, it would help me figure this place out."

"Yeah, but what do you care about me and Danalda?"

"Well," she said, more businesslike, "I figured we could make a deal. You teach me a bit about baseball, and I'll let you in on a few secrets about girls."

"I don't know, Kamna," I said, starting to walk faster.

"Like, for example . . . what's the point of an intentional walk?"

"Well," I said, slowing down my pace, "an intentional walk happens wh—"

I stopped and looked at her hard. I was pretty sure she wasn't messing with me.

"Okay, weirdo," I said, smiling slightly. "I'll try this out. But I'm not making any promises."

"Boy," she said, laughing, "you've got a lot to learn about girls. So what about the intentional walk?"

"It happens when a pitcher throws four balls—you know, pitches outside the strike zone—on purpose. It gives the batter a free pass to first base," I said.

Kamna nodded like she understood.

"There are a number of reasons why a pitcher intentionally walks a batter," I continued. "But the most exciting reason happens when the batter is so good that giving up one base is better than giving up a double, triple, or home run."

"I knew it," she declared, flapping her hands for me to stop talking. "Absolutely perfect . . . Wait . . . let me think for a sec." She looked up to the sky. "Okay. Listen up, Darcy."

"Yeah, sure. Whatever," I said.

"Okay, okay," she said, getting excited again. "You can't tell anyone this, all right?"

I nodded like a gentleman with my hand on the brim of my ball cap.

"All right, you know Teresa what's-her-name?"

"You mean, the blond one or the short one with—?"

"The blond one. Okay, she's in my music class. She plays flute and I play clarinet." She made the two-finger gagging action about playing clarinet. "So she sits a row in front of me, and I heard her saying that Jim, you know, the jerk—but also the best-looking guy in eighth grade—is always coming on strong to her. She said she lets him kiss her as much as he wants so that he won't want to go further."

I was a little embarrassed by the way the conversation was going, but Kamna wasn't.

"So?" I said, trying to sound uninterested.

"Sooooo . . . it's like an intentional walk. She lets him get to first base to keep him from getting to second or further." She did another gag signal.

"Yeah, but it's different," I argued. "He probably thinks he's going to get to second because he got to first so easily. Did you ask her if it works?"

Kamna blinked. "No, it's not like we're best friends or anything. But the point is—"

"I bet it doesn't work!"

"Well, maybe," she said, sighing. "But the point is I just learned something about baseball and you just learned something about girls. You did, didn't you?"

"Yeah," I said. "I learned that some girls don't know anything about guys."

"You're impossible!"

"Maybe," I said, tipping my hat to her. "See ya!"

And before she could respond, I turned the corner, away from my new friend and toward home.

The house was quiet when I got home. I knew Beattie and Sam were doing some spring shopping. I went through the den, half expecting to see Grandpa napping on his favorite chair, his head tilted back, his mouth of dentures wide open. I threw my glove on his chair and was heading to the kitchen for a drink of something when I heard some creaking above my head.

Nap's office is directly above the kitchen, and whenever he shifts in his swivel chair, the wheels roll on the old wooden floor and make the sound of cracking knuckles. I poured a glass of milk and made my way upstairs. Nap was there with his back to me, his feet up on his desk. There was a book on his lap, but he wasn't reading. He was staring out the window at our swaying maple tree.

"Hi, Nap," I said at the doorway.

Nap swung his head my way and smiled, unsurprised. He must have heard me coming up the stairs. "Hi there, Darce. How'd tryouts go today?"

"Not bad. We were only fielding. I bobbled one ball on a bad bounce."

"Good, good," he said absently. "Whatcha up to now?"

"Don't know," I said. "Hey, Nap? Can I ask you a question?"

"Sure."

"Who's Norman Duffy?"

Nap's eyes flickered like flames. "Where did you hear that name?"

"I don't know," I said dishonestly. "I think I heard Grandpa or Sam say it once, and it just got stuck in my brain."

"Huh," Nap said, turning his head back toward the window. He paused long enough that I thought he might not answer. Then his voice got that soft, storytelling tone, the one he used to use when he read storybooks to me. I took a swallow of my milk, leaned my head against the door frame, and listened.

"Norman Duffy," he said, squinting memory-searching eyes back at me, "was about the fattest kid you've ever seen in your life. I know you're not supposed to say that these days, but it was true. He was F-A-T. They say that the kids of today eat too much junk food. Well, Normie, he could have eaten every piece of candy at the store on Station Street. We used to joke that he would have eaten a whole liver if it had a grain of sugar on it. Gobstoppers were his weakness, though. I don't think a day went by when he didn't have six of them, three on either side, making his cheeks look like a chipmunk's. Normie was in my grade, and some of the boys in my class made a sport of trying to pick his bulging pockets for a stopper. If he hadn't been such a funny guy, I think he would have been very unhappy. He always had a way of laughing things off."

"Did he play baseball?"

Nap froze and hardened me with a stare. "Why? Is that what Grandpa said?"

"No . . . I don't know."

He sighed. "Let's talk about it some other time, son."

"Sure," I said, turning to go.

"Hey, Darcy?

"Yeah?"

"Glad to hear it went well today."

"Thanks, Nap."

12

◆

READING THE SIGNS

◆

signal **def.** A movement or gesture performed by a coach or catcher to indicate to a player or pitcher the strategy for the upcoming pitch. Just before a batter steps into the batter's box, he looks up the third-base line to the third-base coach for a signal.

On Tuesday morning, I saw Danalda and Jennifer walking toward my locker. I didn't have time to think. Jennifer ran up in a flurry of tiptoe steps, and Danalda hung back shyly.

"Lab mate," she said cheerily. "I hear you're trying out for the Cheetahs! How exciting!"

Danalda was holding her textbooks on her stomach with her two hands, looking away down the corridor.

"Yeah," I said, trying to sound as positive as possible. "I think my chances are, you know, not bad. I took about ten grounders, and I had no errors. There was one that I bobbled a bit, but it wasn't an err—"

"Did you hit a home run?" Jennifer interrupted.

This caught Danalda's attention.

"Um . . . well . . . no," I stammered. "We didn't have—"

"Oh well, maybe next time, right?" she said, giving me a little punch on the arm. "We gotta go to class. See ya."

"Bye," I said to Jennifer.

"Bye," I said, looking back at Danalda.

She took one hand away from her books and made a short wave. Then she mouthed a soundless "Bye." They sauntered off, and when I was sure they were out of sight, I banged my head lightly on my locker door.

When I saw Kamna in the hallway before lunch, she dug into her pocket and handed me Getting the Girl Rule #2. I grabbed it and read.

Getting the Girl Rule #2:

NOW THAT YOU ARE ON GOOD TERMS WITH JENNIFER, MAKE CONTACT WITH DANALDA WHEN THEY ARE TOGETHER. MAKE SURE IT'S ONLY THE TWO OF THEM—A THIRD GIRL MIGHT THINK YOU ARE A LOSER (SORRY) AND THEN YOU'RE IN TROUBLE. TELL HER ABOUT TRYING OUT FOR THE BASEBALL

TEAM, BUT SAY IT LIKE YOU ARE GOING TO MAKE IT.
DON'T SAY ANYTHING MORE. END THE CONVERSATION.

When I finished, I looked over at Kamna. "Done."

"What do you mean, 'Done'?"

"I mean I saw Danalda and Jennifer this morning, and I told them about all my grounders and how I bobbled one, sort of, and how, well, I didn't get a home run and—"

"Okay," Kamna interrupted as we approached the cafeteria. "So you totally screwed up with the confident-of-making-the-team part, and you blabbed on a bit about the—what do you call them—grounders?"

"What do you mean, I screwed up?" I demanded, waving her over to an empty table in the cafeteria. "It says here"—I flapped Getting the Girl Rule #2 in the air— "to tell her about my try-out with the Cheetahs."

"Read again, Darcy! I said tell her about *trying out* for the Cheetahs, meaning just let her know that it's happening, that you are good enough to be there, not to share all the details."

"I don't get it. The details are the most important things, aren't they?" I said as we both sat down.

"Not when you don't really care about them," she said, then paused. "Okay, ask me what I did this weekend."

"What did you do this weekend?"

"I was trying out for a modeling agency in New York and—"

"You were?"

◆ **87** ◆

"No, we're pretending, goofball. Ask me again."

"Um . . . what did you do this weekend?"

"I was trying out for a modeling agency in New York, and the dress I wore made me look like a pear. My walking was a disaster. I tripped right at the end of the runway. It didn't matter anyway, because everyone else was way more beautiful. One of the girls, Clare, besides having the most stunning curly red hair, is so gorgeo—"

"Okay, okay," I said. "I get it. I'm bored. Absolutely not interested."

"Exactly," Kamna said, smiling. "No blabbing about baseball details. I'm telling you, she doesn't want to know. Now, you told me you said good-bye to Danalda. Like how?"

"Bye," I said, with a couple of short waves.

"Oh, boy," she said, rolling her eyes. "We'll have to work on that. Now, what about her? What did she do?"

I imitated Danalda's wave.

"Oh my gosh," she said. "Just like that. With her four fingers one after another. And she *mouthed* 'Bye.' There was no sound. Are you sure?"

"Yeah, just like that! What's the big deal?"

"The big deal," she declared in an excited whisper, "is that she was giving you some pretty clear signals."

"You mean like when the third-base coach signals for a steal?" I suggested, doing a quick arm slide, ear wiggle, and cap-brim caress.

"Um, I'm not sure," she said, scrunching up her brow. "Let's put it this way, Darcy. Even though you didn't do anything right today—as in *zero*—I think maybe Danalda actually likes you.

"Now," she went on, like an eager student, "who's this third-base coach and what are these signals all about?"

"A signal is what catchers and coaches give. Catchers give signals to pitchers during the game, and the third-base coach gives signals to hitters and runners. Last year on the Twins—"

"The Twins?"

"Yeah, that was my team last year," I explained. "Coach Perkins's son, Alex, was the third-base coach. Alex's job was to give signals to the hitters so that we knew how to swing, and signals to the runners so that we knew when to run. The problem was Alex loved to make really complicated ones. He used his ears, his hat, his chest, his arm, the dirt, and even the side of his foot to get his message across. There is always a key, the signal that means that the next signal is the important one. As soon as you see the key, like his right hand sliding down the right side of his body, the next signal, like his left hand wiggling his left ear, which meant 'bunt,' is the one you are supposed to pay attention to. If there is no key, then the signals mean nothing."

"That's confusing," she said.

"You're telling me," I said. "And to top it all off, Alex was so convinced that other teams were stealing his signals that he changed the key almost every game. We were always looking over at him totally confused."

"Sounds like you when I'm trying to explain girls," she said.

"Funny," I said. "Tell me something I don't know."

"Okay," she said, leaning across the table. "When you are asking a girl out, never call her on the phone if she hasn't already given you her phone number. She might think you are a bit creepy just calling her up out of the blue. Asking for her number is just as dangerous as asking her on a date. Might as well 'swing for the fences'—I heard someone say that yesterday. Ask her when she's alone. Girls are strange when they are together. Danalda might brush you off even if she's just with Jennifer. Think of something fun to do that you know she'll like."

"Like a movie," I said.

"No, not for your first date. Save that for later. It's too dark, and there's no time to talk."

"Talk? What about—"

"Just do what I say, Darce," she interrupted. "Now that I think of it, Danalda is in my English class in third period in Room 215, but none of her friends are. She never talks to anyone, and she always rushes out when the bell rings. I'll try to distract her for a moment at the door. Make sure you are there outside the door right after third period tomorrow."

"But I don't think I can—"

"Look, I gotta go practice my clarinet scales," she said. "Good luck, Mr. Baseball."

Dwight called that night. We hadn't had a chance to talk since the first tryout. While I'd been waiting to replace Sherman on the field, I saw Dwight miss an easy pop fly. This was a disaster.

If he wasn't fielding well, his chances of making the team were absolute zero.

"I'm finished," he declared. "Done. I pulled a Snodgrass and missed the ball. My career is over. I'm not even going to show up for the tryout on Friday."

"Come on, Dwight," I said. "It couldn't have been that bad. What did Yogi Berra say? 'It's not over till—'"

"Not that bad? Not over?" he squealed. "I missed the easiest pop fly in the world and overthrew the catcher by ten feet."

"Still," I said.

"Still nothing. I'd be lucky if they let me take the field next tryout." He sighed. "How'd it go for you?"

"I only bobbled one grounder, but I think Coach Rizzuto was going pretty easy on us."

"Still, that's pretty good," he said. "I thought I saw you turn a nice double play."

"Yeah, thanks. It was just a flick to second."

"By the way," Dwight said, "I saw Ralph in the hallway today. He asked how the tryout went. Told me you hung up on him. Nice work. That guy is acting strange these days. Anyway, he told me he made *Dracula*. He's the fly-eating guy."

"Perfect," we said in unison.

"Hey," he said, his voice changing. "I forgot to tell you. I watched the end of Beattie's game at the small diamond last week, and after the game, I was talking to Dave—you know, the guy who runs the girls' softball league—and he said he had just lost an ump. He said if I worked a couple of games and got my umpiring certificate, I could be a substitute for Little League. So yesterday, I umpired a game. It was wicked. *Steeeee-rike one!* Man, can I ever call a strike." He paused. "Dave asked if I could umpire on Friday."

"What'd you say?"

"Um," Dwight said. "Yes."

"What about the Cheetahs tryout?" I demanded.

"I don't have a chance, Darcy. Everybody knows that."

I was silent. I felt abandoned.

"Beattie told me about Grandpa Spillman," Dwight said. "Too bad, Darce. Where'd they put him?"

"Some stupid home. Look, I gotta go, Dwight."

"Okay, Darce," he said. "Just . . . keep your eye on the ball."

"Always do," I said, and hung up the phone.

Dwight seemed to be doing better than both Ralph and me. He was playing within himself.

13

◆

HOLDING BACK ON A PITCH

◆

check swing **def.** A half swing of the bat, stopped before the batter turns over his wrists. If a batter "check swings" on a pitch that is outside the strike zone, it is called a ball, not a strike.

In third-period Spanish on Wednesday, it was like I was settling my feet in the batter's box. Instead of practicing my verbs, I planned how I was going to get to the second floor to intercept Danalda. My class was on the first floor, but it was in Room 117, almost directly below Danalda and Kamna's English class. With five minutes to go, I slid my books into my knapsack, and with a less than a minute to go, I got up, acting like I was going up to ask Mrs. Gomez a question. Just before I got to her desk, I looked at my watch and veered toward the door.

The bell drowned out Mrs. Gomez's "Where do you think you are going?" I slipped out the door, tore down the hallway, and started to climb. The stairs were crowded, so I had to slalom through people all the way up. I almost ran straight into Simone, Ralph's ex-girlfriend, who squealed as we stopped within inches of each other. I apologized and ran on. When I got to the second floor, I could see that 215's door was still closed. I slowed to a walk, catching my breath as I waited by the lockers across from the room.

I heard the rumble of chairs and feet inside the classroom, then the door swung open. Danalda was the first to exit, followed by Kamna. Danalda was moving fast, her head down, her books tight to her chest. I took a step forward, but then saw Kamna's waving arms. She was doing the "safe" signal, slicing the air with her hands, and she was mouthing the word "No." I took another step toward Danalda, but Kamna's movements became frantic. She fell forward as other students pushed out of the class. I glared at her silently until Danalda was out of range.

"What was that all about?" I demanded.

"Believe me," she said, "you didn't want to ask her today. Danalda had a *baaaaad* class. Gotta go. I'll tell you at lunch. Mr. Wurst locks the door if you are late."

I noticed Thelma giving Kamna and me a weird look as we scurried over to the opposite corner of the cafeteria at the beginning of lunch. It was the second time that we had talked alone, two too many times with detectives like Thelma around.

"Tell Thelma you like Ralph," I said after taking a bite of my peanut butter sandwich.

"What?"

"She keeps on looking over here. Tell her you like Ralph and you are asking me questions."

"Thelma?" she said, laughing. "Don't worry about Thelma."

"What are you going to say we're talking about? Baseball?"

"Sure," she said. "Why not?"

I scowled at her. "All right, all right. Then tell her you used the 'safe' signal to stop me from asking Danalda on a date."

"It was the Big Disaster Ahead signal!"

"Whatever," I said. "In baseball, when you put your hands flat together in front of you, then take them apart, it means 'safe.' The runner is safe."

"Okay, I get it. Thanks, Mr. Baseball. Now can I tell you what happened in the real world?"

I wiggled my right ear with my hand, ran my right hand down my left arm, and then coughed three times.

"I'm assuming that's the signal for 'yes.'"

I shrugged with a smirk. "Swing away."

"Well, Danalda didn't have her homework done, and Mrs. Charles was in a bad mood. Danalda whispered over to this girl Frances, who always has her work done, but Frances totally ignored her. I saw it all go down. Danalda was fuming. When Mrs. Charles asked her for the answer, she looked up with this pathetic, blank face. Later, I saw Danalda whispering something to Frances. It didn't sound very nice."

"So what was the deal stopping me like that?" I said.

"Look," she said. "There's no way you want to ask Danalda on a date when she's in a mood like that. To be honest, I wonder if you might have the wrong impression of her. I've already told you that she has a real mean streak. One thing's for sure: Danalda doesn't like getting embarrassed."

"Well, who does?" I said testily. I didn't want to admit it, but I didn't like what I was hearing about Danalda. Still, I'd never seen her be mean. I couldn't give up on her from plain hearsay.

"Jeez," I said finally. "I didn't know the planets had to be aligned for me to ask a girl on a date. I thought it was just a matter of stepping in the batter's box and taking a swing."

"Well, it's not," she said, smiling. "Brighten up, Darcy. It's only one strike. You've got two more left, don't you?"

"No way," I said. "It was a bad pitch, and I didn't go around. It was a check swing."

"Check swing?"

"Yeah," I said. "Check swing."

There was no way I was taking a strike for what happened. The ball was coming, I held back just in time, and it veered down the hallway out of the strike zone.

COUNT: 1 ball, 0 strikes (or 1 and 0).

14

◆

SWINGING FOR
THE FENCES

◆

a big cut **def.** A powerful swing that is often meant to hit
the ball over the fence for a home run.

Danalda and Jennifer walked by my locker again on Thursday
morning before class. No "Getting the Girl" instruction had
fallen out of my locker, so I was on my own. I'd spent the whole
night finishing up my comparative English essay ("Ty Cobb vs.
Tony Gwynn: Who Was the Better Hitter?") and studying my
Spanish verbs, and I was tired. I was tired, all right—tired of
being shy and not understanding girls, tired of my boring junior
high life.

I took a big cut.

"Oh, hey there," I said, waving (a short, swift one like Kamna
told me). "What's up?"

"Hey, Darcy," Jennifer said, walking over. Danalda didn't have a chance to hang back this time, but she didn't say a word.

I tried to shift my gaze to Danalda, but I ended up looking slightly cross-eyed between the two of them. "I was wondering if you . . . um . . . you'd come to the Cheetah tryout tomorrow afternoon, and maybe afterward we could—"

"Um . . . Darcy?" Jennifer said, moving her head into my view. "Sure, we'd love to. That'd be fun. Right, Dannie? When is it?"

"Um . . . right after school tomorrow. It'll take about an hour. Then we could—"

"Sure, sure," Jennifer interrupted again. "We'll be there. Right, Dannie?"

Then it happened. Danalda looked me straight in the eyes.

"Sure," she said. "I don't know much about baseball, though."

"We gotta go," Jennifer cut in.

"Sure, fine, see ya then," I said with the last remaining oxygen in my lungs.

Sam and I decided to visit Grandpa on Thursday while Nap took Beattie to her softball game. I hadn't told anyone, not even Beattie, about my visit to Grandpa the weekend before, and I was beginning to worry that Marion might say something about it. When we got to the front desk, she was on the phone. She looked down at the log, nodded, and waved us on. I was a little bit nervous about seeing Grandpa, so it helped that Sam led the way.

"Hello, Grandpa," Sam said cheerfully as she swung open the door.

He was in a chair beside his bed. "Oh, hello there! I was just . . . um . . . um . . . "

"Watching TV?" Sam asked. There was a yellow stickie on the bottom of the screen that read "TV."

"Right, right." He clicked it off with the remote and looked over at me. "And who's this in the Twins hat?"

I was wearing my Little League cap.

"It's me, Darcy," I said. "But I'm trying out for the Cheetahs now."

"Right, right," he said, shaking his head. He lowered his eyes at me like he used to. "Are you playing 'ready'?"

"A step and a dive from the line," I stated. "And up closer for a bunt."

"When does a bunt happen?"

"One time it happens is when there's a runner on first and no out. That way, even if the bunter is thrown out at first, the runner is advanced to second and is in scoring position."

"That's my boy! Come sit here and tell me how your hitting is going."

Sam winked at me and said, "I think I'll let you two talk. Back in a minute."

I sat on the bed beside Grandpa, my glove on my hand.

"Let me see that leather you've got there!"

He grabbed the glove, put it on, and did a few soft glove punches.

"Oh, that feels good," he said, smiling. "I haven't worn a glove in ages. So how's my Babe Ruth hitting these days?"

"Tomorrow's our first hitting tryout."

"Okay," he said. "Remember: Elbows up, small step, follow through."

"Always do," I said. "Hey, Grandpa?"

"Yes, son."

I needed to take advantage of this time alone. "I sort of asked that girl out on a date."

Grandpa's eyes bulged. "Woohee!" he cried, slapping his glove-less hand on his knee. "What's her name?"

"Danalda."

"You like her?"

"I think so."

"She play baseball?"

"Most beautiful swing I've ever seen."

Grandpa slapped his leg again. "What about that other girl . . . Mary?"

"You mean Thelma?"

"No, Mary. The one you took to the prom."

"You mean Thelma at the Valentine's Dance?"

Grandpa stared at me. "No! Mary, you know, Mary."

His voice was getting tense.

"Who?" Sam said. She must have slipped in while we were talking.

Grandpa looked up at her angrily. "Mary!"

"It's okay, Grandpa. We didn't mean to get you upset," she said, walking up and putting her hand on my shoulders. "Darcy and I just wanted to say a quick hello. You need some rest."

When I reached for the glove, it fell softly out of Grandpa's limp hand.

"See ya, Grandpa."

"Bye," he said, looking out the window at nothing.

"Darcy," Sam said, once we were in the car, heading back home. "In all the confusion these last couple of months, your dad and I haven't had a chance to talk to you about Grandpa."

I just stared out the car window.

"We think the reason why Grandpa's been acting strange is—"

"Grandpa's acting fine," I said, still looking away.

"Darcy," she said nicely, "Grandpa is a bit sick. He might have—"

"I know exactly what Grandpa's got. He's got put-in-a-retirement-home-and-abandoned-by-his-family syndrome."

"Darcy Jonathan!" Sam shouted, swerving slightly on the road.

"Tell me it isn't true, Mom! We stuck him in there 'cause we didn't want to deal with him anymore."

Sam didn't say anything. We drove in silence all the way home.

As I was getting out of the car, Sam reached over. "I know this is hard, Darcy. Anytime you want to talk about it, I'm . . . we're here."

15

◆

FOUL TIPS

◆

foul ball **def.** A batted ball that lands in foul territory beyond
first or third base or arrives in foul territory before passing
first or third base. A foul counts as a strike unless it's the last
one. A batter can only strike out on a foul if it's a bunt. If it
pops up or is ticked, the ball can be caught for an out.

When Coach Rizzuto was speaking to the group on the mound
on Friday, Danalda and Jennifer were nowhere to be seen.

"All right, boys," Coach Rizzuto said. "Here's . . . what you've
all been waiting for. Batting practice! I want the following players to take . . . the field while we do BP."

Coach Rizzuto called out all of the best players, including
Sherman. It was depressing to see what looked like the final team

jog out to their positions, smiling and joking with one another. The rest of us sized one another up, knowing that we would be scrambling for the handful of backup positions. When Coach Rizzuto told the rest of us to line up for batting order, I jumped quickly into the front of the line. I knew the fielders would eventually have to switch in to bat, and I wanted every chance to be the one to swap with them. At fourth in the order, I had a good chance of being asked to field later on.

While I was in the hole, I scanned the bleachers behind the backstop, which were scattered with a few enthusiastic parents. There was no sign of the girls. When Greg Harwood finished hitting, I moved into the on-deck circle, picked up a bat with a weight ring on it, and took some slow, heavy practice swings. Coach Rizzuto was pitching some straight-ahead fastballs, so I took the ring off the bat to time my swings with the speed of his throws. I took a big cut and heard a familiar voice in the distance.

"Let's go, you big Darcy in there!"

Without turning, I knew it was Ralph.

I smiled, looking up the hill on the third-base line. When I saw who Ralph was with, the smile vanished from my face. Danalda and Jennifer were sitting on either side of him at the top of the hill.

"Okay. Let's go, Spillman," Coach Rizzuto hollered from the mound. It was my turn.

I connected on every pitch Coach Rizzuto threw me. The

problem was that most of the connections were foul tips into the backstop, dribbles to the coach, and big hops to the infield.

"That's all right, Darcy!" Coach Rizzuto barked. "Get the rust . . . out."

On the next pitch, I sent a hard liner to third base, straight into Sherman's glove. Sherman smiled and cockily kicked the dirt in front of him.

"One more," Coach Rizzuto said.

I stepped slowly back into the batter's box, leading with my left foot, settling it in, then placing my right foot down. Coach Rizzuto wound up.

It was a hard fastball down the middle. I swung a bit late, but I heard the soft-spot sound, and I knew it was good one. When you hit the soft spot, even though you've crushed the ball, you barely feel the vibration of the bat in your hands. The ball flies like from a spring. When I first sighted the ball, a white blur to my left, it was high in the air past Sherman's outstretched glove. The ball was curving gently, heading for both the fence and foul territory. The speedy left fielder, Freddie Chaplin, was chasing it down, trying to make one of his spectacular plays. The ball hit the ground ten feet before the fence, just out of reach of Fred's glove, just outside the third-base line.

Foul ball.

"Wow, that was an awesome hit at the end there!" Jennifer said at the end of tryouts. I found the three of them—Jennifer, Danalda, and Ralph—still sitting on the hill.

"It was a foul ball," I said gloomily.

"Still," Ralph said, raising his eyebrows, "you didn't make any errors when you got in the field."

"Still, nothing," I said. "No one even hit the ball to me."

I knew Kamna had said to be positive, but I couldn't help myself. The truth was the truth.

Danalda was quiet, but I noticed she was sneaking glances over at me.

"Hey," Ralph said, getting up. "Dannie and Jennie say they're going to the mallie. Wanna come?"

Danalda giggled.

I couldn't believe it—Ralph was stealing my date.

"Nah," I said with fake cheer. "Something came up. I gotta go home."

"You sure?" Danalda asked, her face suddenly changing.

"Um . . . yeah," I said. "Maybe next time. Sorry."

I waved and walked past them. I strode away like I was in a hurry, although I was hoping unrealistically that Danalda would come after me.

Just as I got onto Station Street, I heard footsteps. It was Ralph.

"Hey, stop," he said, panting. "You training to be a speed walker or something?" He did the funny-looking, hip-swivel speed walk past me.

I didn't even crack a smile.

He looked over his shoulder. "Why don't you come with us? This is your big chance, Darce-man. Danalda looks upset that you aren't coming."

I shrugged my shoulders and kept on walking.

"All right," he said. "Miss the chance of a lifetime!"

"Okay," I said, and left him standing still.

I couldn't help myself. I didn't want Ralph to steal my thunder, and besides, I didn't want to go on a date with Danalda after such a crappy tryout. Everything seemed to be going great with her until the very last second—just like with my slightly curving foul-ball strike.

COUNT: 1 ball and 1 strike (or 1 and 1).

16

◆

STEPPING OUT OF
THE BATTER'S BOX

◆

dust in the eye **def.** Many professionals raise their hand to
the umpire, pretending they have gotten dust in their eye,
and step out of the batter's box. A batter does this before
the pitcher's windup begins, as a way of stopping the game
temporarily. The pitcher's rhythm and concentration are dis-
turbed, and the batter gains an advantage.

I called Kamna after dinner on Friday, but her mother answered
again, saying she couldn't talk because of homework. A half hour
later, Kamna did call, whispering.

"Can you meet me tomorrow?" she breathed.

"What's with the whispering?"

"Meet me at the little diamond at ten in the morning."

"In the morning?" I griped. "But I'm watching the late movie—"

"Gotta go. See ya there."

The next morning, we were sitting on the bleachers, staring out across the empty diamond. Kamna explained that because she had recently gotten 87 percent on a math test, which was a low mark in her household, her parents were being particularly strict. When I told her about the recent developments in the Danalda situation, she had some criticism.

"From the outside, it looks like you totally screwed up," she stated.

I was slowly getting used to Kamna's bluntness.

"But in a way, what you did was . . . was . . . accidentally ingenious. Perfect, even. Now all you have to do is avoid her for a couple days."

"Avoid her?" I said, exasperated. "I'm running out of time here. Next Thursday is the last tryout."

"I know, I know. Just a couple of days," she insisted. "Hey, isn't there a time in a baseball game that you kind of delay a bit to get your . . . opponent . . . thinking?"

"Yeah," I said. "I guess so. The batter steps out of the box."

"The box?"

I pointed to the small rectangular boxes on either side of home plate.

"Okay, that's good," she said pensively. "By not going to the mall with Danalda, it was like you were stepping out of the box. Now you've got to stay out of the box as long as possible so that the bowler—sorry, that's cricket—the pitcher, you know, Danalda, has to think. I know this sounds mad, but Danalda is probably more interested in you because you didn't go to the mall with her. What you did is called 'playing hard to get.' Isn't that from baseball?"

"It sounds like it, but it's not . . . and if by mad you mean crazy, that sounds pretty accurate."

Kamna's forehead went wrinkly. She was already on to another thought. "Why *didn't* you go to the mall? Didn't *you* invite *them* out to the tryout?"

"Yeah, I did," I said, squinting across the field. "I don't know. I guess I was so ticked off about my batting, and about how Danalda and Jennifer didn't understand that a foul ball is not a hit . . . and that Ralph knew it hadn't gone well but was pretending it had."

I looked over, and before I knew it, I found myself saying, "I also kind of wanted to be alone because I was angry at my parents about putting my grandpa into a retirement home."

"Whoa!" she said, shaking her head in disbelief. "We don't do that where I come from. My mother would never put my grandmother in a home."

"It was more Nap than Sam, but I guess both of them deci—"

"Who are Nap and Sam?"

"Nap's my dad . . . it's for Napoleon. And Sam is for Samantha. She's my mom."

"Weeeeeird," Kamna said. "My father doesn't even let me call him Dad. Just Father."

"Weeeeeird," I mimicked. "I guess it doesn't matter what you call them, though. They still pull some major SPMs."

"SPMs? Let me guess, another baseball statistic?"

"No," I said. "But my friend Dwight *did* make it up. Stupid Parent Maneuvers. Whenever one of our parents does something idiotic, we call it an SPM."

"If not letting me use the phone counts as an SPM, then my mom is the queen," she said, leaning back on the bleachers and looking at the cottony clouds above. "Why'd they put him in the home?"

"Oh, I don't know," I said, kicking a stone off the bleacher. "Nap and Grandpa don't always get along, but I don't think that was it." I paused. "He sort of started doing weird things, like suddenly disappearing and turning the oven on in the middle of the day . . . with nothing in it. Sometimes I think he thinks I'm Nap. He keeps on talking about this baseball game that he thinks I played in."

"Oh," she said. "I'm sorry, Darcy. It sounds like he's got something like Alzheimer's."

"Alzheimer's?" I breathed it to myself a few times. "I think I've heard that somewhere, but I don't think he has a disease. He's just old."

"My mom's best friend's mother had it," she said, her nose

wrinkling. "It was kind of funny in a sad way . . . if you know what I mean."

I thought of Grandpa demanding his coconut donuts at Zak's and nodded.

"She totally denied that my mom's friend was her daughter. She would say, 'You are a very nice person, but my daughter is much more beautiful. She has a mole on her right cheek and she lives in Calcutta.' The family took it as a joke at first, but it turned out she really thought her daughter was someone else. Once or twice a week, she would get caught in the middle of the night calling the operator for her daughter in Calcutta."

"Whoa! Now, that's weird. What happened to her?"

"That was last year. As far as I know, she stayed in the house. That's the way we do it—family stays with family. Like take my older sister, Pryha, for example. She is thinking of getting married to this guy Donald. He's as white as white can be, which my parents aren't crazy about. If he does ask her to marry him, she's told him they'll have to live with our parents until they get steady jobs."

"I would never do that," I said. "What does Donald think?"

"I don't know," she said, sitting up and shrugging. "Dee— that's what we call him—he's pretty chilled. . . . And my sister is not! She's more traditional than I am."

"Well, when I leave home after high school, it's for good. *Adiós. Ciao.* I'm gone," I said. "You're not going to live with your parents, are you?"

"I'm not sure. . . . I mean, it's hard. My parents' brains are kind of still back in India. And it feels like mine is still sort of . . . "

"In between?"

"Yeah," she laughed. "Somewhere over the Atlantic Ocean. Anyway, I've pretty much been at the top of the class in every subject since I came here—otherwise I'd suffer the wrath of my parents." She paused to think. "My problem is fitting in. . . . Coolness and good grades don't seem to mix too well."

"Yeah, neither do foul balls and girls," I said.

"That's the wrong attitude," she said sternly. "Danalda doesn't know the difference . . . and now that we're talking about it, neither do I."

"It's the difference between me making the team or not," I said. "There's only one more tryout before Coach Rizzuto makes his final cut."

"Okay, back up," Kamna said. "Explain this foul ball thing again. In cricket, the pitch—you know, the field—is a big circle, and you bat in the middle. It's three hundred and sixty degrees around."

I hopped off the bleachers without a word, waving Kamna around to the backstop. I talked her through an at-bat and basically blabbed about baseball—my favorite thing in the world to do.

That night, Nap found me in my room pretending to study. I was just starting to read a book about Mike Schmidt, the Philadelphia Phillies Hall of Fame third baseman. Nap had not vis-ited my room in weeks, and his standing there in my doorway gave me a bit of a fright. He stood there silently, just staring for a moment like he was stuck. Nap didn't seem to notice that I wasn't studying—parents have a way of forgetting the rules when they have something else on their minds. This, it seemed, was one of those times.

"Hey, Darcy." He smiled absently. "How's it going?"

I closed my book slowly. "Not bad."

"When do you find out about the team?"

"Next tryout's the last," I said glumly. "Then I'll get a letter."

"Oh," he said, walking over to my desk chair. He sat down, grabbed my math text, and began to flip through it idly. Nap used to help me with my homework when I was younger, espe-cially with math and science. He would sit beside me as I worked through problems, leaning back and sighing when I started get-ting it wrong. We spent many frustrated hours at that desk, elbow to elbow, me fighting over equations, Nap fighting for them.

Nap finally spoke. "Sam was saying you had a talk . . . well, you didn't have a talk . . . and I thought maybe you might want to have one. About Grandpa."

I looked away.

There was a long silence.

"Sometimes," Nap finally said, putting the math book down gently, "it's easy for us grown-ups to think that you kids understand everything that's going on. We forget that there are things that haven't been explained and that they need explaining. . . . Like once upon a time, I was your age and your grandpa was a young father—"

"No kidding," I snapped. No matter how badly I wanted to hear what he was going to say, I couldn't help myself.

Nap's cheeks went red, and his jaw clenched. I was expecting him to yell at me, but he just sat there, his hand on my textbook.

"Your mother and I have both tried to speak to you like an adult," he said calmly. "We might not have made all the right decisions all of the time, but we do not deserve this . . . this . . . new attitude of yours." He stood and put his hands on his hips. "When you are ready to talk without that tone of voice, we—your mother and I—are here. You understand?"

I couldn't move. I wanted to say that I was ready listen, but it wasn't true. I wanted to say that I would try to understand why they had sent Grandpa away, but I couldn't. I wanted to say I could be an adult about it all, but the fact was I wasn't.

17

◆

GETTING
MIXED SIGNALS

◆

balk **def.** When a pitcher's illegal motion attempts to fool
a base runner into thinking that he is going to pitch the ball
instead of trying to throw the runner out on the base paths.

The balk is one of the most confusing rules in baseball. Here's one
way it can happen: Imagine a runner on first and a left-handed
pitcher starting his motion and stretching his leg toward home
plate. If his leg is more in the direction of the catcher than the
first baseman, but he still throws over to first base to pick off a
base runner, it is considered unfair and illegal and therefore called
a balk. All runners get a free base—in this case, the runner at first
would go to second. A balk can be very dangerous because if there
is a man on third, the runner gets a free pass home for a run.

In science class on Monday, we started a new unit, and Jennifer and I were no longer in same lab group. At the end of class, I hurried out the door so I wouldn't have to talk to Jennifer—I still felt weird about not going to the mall. As I turned down the hall, someone grabbed my arm. It was Danalda, her oddly strong grip on my forearm.

Danalda slid her hand off me and smiled. "Sorry, I didn't mean to scare you. I just wanted to catch you before you ran off. I was wondering . . . what you are doing this Saturday?"

I got lost in the swirl of her bluish-gray eyes.

I blinked. Could it be true? Was Danalda asking me out? What was I supposed to do? Kamna had not prepared me for this.

"Um . . . I'm not sure," I said, going with the friendly-but-distant thing.

Danalda shifted a little and looked over my shoulder.

"Well, I mean," she said quickly. "I was just wondering . . . It's not important. Forget it."

"No, no," I said, feeling like a complete idiot. "It's just that I need to . . . find out—"

"You've got other plans? It's fine. No problem," she said, but her face was bright red.

"Umm . . . No . . . I mean, yeah . . . How about I give you a call? I just . . . I need to . . . you know . . . like you said, find out about whether I've got to do what I've got to do . . . if you know what I mean."

"Fine. Whatever. My number is 555-9801," she said coldly. "I gotta get to class."

"Um . . . 555-9801 . . . Yeah, okay," I stammered. "I'll . . . I'll call you."

For the rest of school, I couldn't think straight. Had I been a complete idiot? Was Danalda even asking me on a date? Wasn't she undoing her question even before I could answer? The more I thought about it, I realized she hadn't even thrown the ball. She'd stepped toward home plate to deliver her pitch, but the ball never came.

Danalda had balked.

Kamna didn't buy the balk explanation when I called her that night. Her parents were at the movies.

"You said what? 'Um, I'm not sure'?" she gasped. "What did she do?"

"It was weird," I said. "She went all red like she was angry."

"I'll bet," Kamna said. "Danalda's not used to being turned down." She paused. "So why didn't you say yes?"

"You said to stay away from her!"

"But that was so that she would be more interested and *you* could ask *her* on a date. It's like you caught a fish without a rod and then you threw it back in the water. Wait. I take that back—I'm beginning to sound like my father. Danalda is no fish. You are no fisherman. And that was no balk . . . at least as far as you've explained it."

"That's wonderful, but listen," I said defensively. "It was totally a balk. Danalda was asking me out . . . I think . . . but she didn't come through with it. It's like maybe she wants to walk me on to first base instead of taking a chance and giving me a juicy pitch to swing at. The count is definitely one ball and one strike. One and one."

"You aren't *actually* pretending this is an at-bat, are you?"

"Of course I am! It's one and one, a good pitch to get a hit on. Not as good as two and one or three and one, the hitter's pitch, but pretty smackin' good."

"You are mad, Darcy. Absolutely mad. You know that, don't you?"

"And I'm supposed to take that as a compliment?"

There was a pause. "Well, let's just say I get why Danalda likes you. You are funny, bright, and . . . and . . ."

"Absolutely handsome," I said sarcastically.

"No," she said, her voice no longer the same. "Let's say unique-looking."

"Unique-looking?" I said. "That doesn't sound like a compliment."

"Well, it's all you're going to get."

"Fine," I said. "What do you think my chances are with Danalda?"

There was another, even longer pause. "Either she hates your guts now or she wants you even more."

"I don't want her to go out with me because I played hard to get."

"We don't always get what we want, Darcy." She paused. "I gotta go."

"Thanks," I said to the dial tone and hung up the phone.

COUNT: 1 and 1.

18

◆

CONFERENCE
ON THE SIDELINES

◆

go down swinging vs. go down looking **def.** In baseball, there
are two ways to strike out. If you *go down looking*, the
pitcher has thrown the ball in the strike zone for the third
strike, and you have not swung. If you *go down swinging*,
you have swung through the pitch and struck out.

I found Ralph at his locker just before lunch on Tuesday. Because
we aren't in the same classes and don't have lockers on the same
floor, we don't bump into each other much if we don't mean to.

"Hey," I said.

"Hey," he replied, looking into his locker. "What's Darcy
Spillman doin' on the third floor corral? Ropin' cattle?"

Ralph threw in a jokey, cowboy accent, but he wasn't going to
get cheap laughs. I didn't say anything.

"Look, Darce-man, I'm sorry about that phone conversation way back," he said, still looking in his locker.

Ralph had never apologized to me for anything.

"And what about telling Kamna about my theory?" I said.

Ralph's face went red. "Me and my big mouth. I was sort of trying to help. Look, Darce. I'm really, really sorry about everything. I didn't know about Grandpa S—Dwight told me—but that's no excuse. I shouldn't have said anything to Kamna. You remember what Mr. Davies put on my report card last year." He plugged his nose so that his voice went like a horn. "Ralph is spontaneous and impulsive, which rarely benefits either him or his classmates."

I had to laugh this time. Ralph did a great Mr. Davies voice.

"It's okay, I guess," I said. "Things have been pretty messed up for the three of us this year. Dwight's in La-La Land with Liam, and I haven't exactly been the sanest guy in the world. . . . And now you could say I'm in a bit of a pickle."

His eyes brightened. "Between first and second or second and third?"

"Um . . . between home plate and first."

Ralph rubbed his hands together and giggled evilly. "Sounds interestingly impossible. Just my kind of problem. What can I do?"

"Tell you what," I said. "I haven't had a Gravy Mountain in ages. I'll split a basket with ya if I can pick your brain."

Ralph and I made our way to the cafeteria, and when we

finally sat down with the fries, I threw Kamna's final letter on the table.

"What's this?" Ralph asked.

"Just open it up, and if you laugh . . . I'll kill you!" I said, having a couple of fries.

Ralph snatched it off the table with glee.

Final Piece of Advice:

YOU'VE GOT TO FORGET THE WHOLE AT-BAT THING. THIS IS NOT A BASEBALL GAME. IF YOU ARE THE BATTER, AND DANALDA IS THE PITCHER, THEN WHO AM I? THE UMPIRE? NO THANKS. IF YOU WANT TO GO OUT WITH DANALDA, JUST ASK HER. I THINK MAYBE THIS IS WHERE I STOP GIVING ADVICE. I'VE LEARNED ENOUGH ABOUT BASEBALL TO KNOW THAT I DON'T WANT TO LEARN ANY MORE. THANKS FOR THE COACHING ANYWAY. K

P.S. I MIGHT NOT KNOW ENOUGH ABOUT BASEBALL, BUT I DO KNOW HEAPS ABOUT GIRLS. IF DANALDA IS A PITCHER, THEN SHE GAVE YOU A SPOT-ON PITCH YESTERDAY. BUT YOU DIDN'T EVEN SWING, DARCY. IF YOU INSIST ON THE BASEBALL COUNT, THEN IT IS 1 AND 2, NOT 1 AND 1. MY FINAL PIECE OF ADVICE: SWING NEXT TIME.

While Ralph read, his face contorted, his eyebrows furrowed, his lips went taut. His gaze stopped at the bottom of the note.

He didn't look up for a while. Ralph was doing something I had never seen him do: composing himself.

"Okay," he said slowly. "I know I can be a blabbermouth jerk about these sorts of things, so I am going to do my best not to be . . . but I can't make any promises."

I couldn't expect more from him. "Fine."

"All right," he said, putting one hand on the table to brace himself. "What the snotballs is this?"

"Well, remember what you said about baseball and girls?"

"Not this again?"

"Well, I think I've taken it a little too far." I took a deep breath. "I am trying to use my baseball knowledge and Cheetah tryouts to help me get to first base with Danalda. I wasn't doing so well with it, so when you told Kamna about my theory, we sort of decided she'd help me figure it out, but as you can see she's out of the game, and now I don't really know what to do."

Ralph winced.

"What?" I said defensively. "You know, you said we had to take advantage of our baseball before it was too late. You said, 'They don't call it getting to first base for nothin'.'"

"Okay, okay," Ralph said with both hands in front of him. "So what's this one-and-two business?"

"That's the count," I said earnestly. "At least that's what Kamna thinks it is."

"For what?" he said, raising one eyebrow. "Getting to first base with Danalda?"

I nodded.

Ralph's eyes bulged.

"Okay," he finally gasped. "First of all, before we go any further here, I've got to say this for the record. You are *totally twisted*! Like, completely messed in the brain! Wait . . . wait . . . don't interrupt. But I've gotta say this much. This baseball idea of yours is . . . is . . . is . . . the greatest, wackiest, most ragingest thing I've ever heard of in my life."

He laughed, hitting his palm on the table. "Here I am trying to figure out how to get as far as possible with a girl and you are counting balls and strikes to just kiss one. You kill me, Darcy-boy. Meanwhile, this Kamna girl," he said, holding up the note. "I think she likes you."

"Whatever," I retorted.

"Okay. Forget Kamna," he said, leaning in. "What's with Danalda? I'm going to need to know absolutely everything."

I explained it all, from getting on Jennifer's side to calling Danalda's balk. Ralph listened, but looked like he was going to burst.

"That Kamna knows what she's talking about," he said, finally grabbing a fry and eating it. "Heck, even I learned a couple of things there! She was especially right about the non-balk call. That was a strike if I've ever seen one. But it's okay . . . you've just taken a juicy fastball down the middle, and you'll know what to do with it next time. Man! This is the majors, Darcy-boy. The majors. I've got to think about it for a bit, but I believe I can put together a few hitting tips for you."

Ralph found me in the hallway the next morning and handed me a note.

THE WORD on Asking a Girl Out
by Ralph Peterson, Esq.

1. Take her to a movie. They are the best—no awkward silences and better chances for getting to first base. Scary movies are the ultimate—unless, of course, they scare you, in which case, they are the worst.

2. Be confident. ("So, you want to go out on Friday?" not "I was wondering if you might deem it possible to go out sometime in the next decade?")

3. Go in with a plan. ("So, we'll go to *Teen Terror IV* on Friday," not "Um, I'm not sure. What would you like to do?") If she can't think of anything, you're finished!

4. Ask her alone. If she says no, you'll want no witnesses.

5. Stand up straight, Darcy. That slouch of yours will get you nowhere fast.

I found Danalda alone at her locker on Wednesday.

"Hi there," I said. "Sorry about earlier this week . . . I was, like, totally spaced."

She looked at me sideways, committing nothing.

"Um . . . so . . . I was wondering"—trying to follow Ralph's rules was like throwing with the wrong arm—"you want to go to *Suspended* on Friday?"

"I was thinking *Between the Lines*," she said, turning with a sudden smile. "Jennifer and Michael are going to come. . . . We'll meet at the corner of Station and Third at six-thirty."

It was like she was expecting this. It was all too easy. I could almost hear Kamna saying, "Danalda likes it when she gets what she wants."

"Um . . . sure . . . great," I said, thinking.

Ralph's rules were quickly out the window. At least we were alone.

I stood up taller. "Six-thirty at Station and Third. Yep, I can do that. No problem."

"Great," she said, touching my arm softly. "I gotta go. See you there."

I didn't move as I dazedly watched Danalda walk away. I couldn't believe it: I was actually going on a date with Danalda Chase, one of the coolest, most beautiful girls in the school. I knew I was supposed to feel completely pumped about it, but somehow I didn't. Then again, maybe it made sense—I still had some serious work ahead of me. After all, you don't throw your arms in the air when you think you just hit a single. No, you don't even watch where the ball goes. You just put your head down and run as hard as you can to first base.

NEW COUNT: 1 and 2.

19

◆

THE SWEET SPOT

◆

to connect **def.** To really hit the ball solidly.

At the final tryout for the Cheetahs on Thursday afternoon, Coach Rizzuto spoke to us gravely.

"This is . . . the final tryout, boys. Congratulations to all . . . of you. Everyone has given their all. Unfortunately, some of you . . . here won't make the team this year. Remember, there are a few baseball professionals who at one point were cut from a team. Never give up on your dreams, boys. All right, let's . . . play ball!"

After some throwing and running warm-ups, Coach Rizzuto made two teams with the players that remained. A number of players, like Dwight, had given up their hopes of making the team and had not shown up for the final, so we were down from thirty players to about twenty, just over two full teams. One team consisted of the probable starters, Sherman Smith and the like; the other was the group of hopefuls. The hopefuls took the field first, and Coach Rizzuto put me at third. This was a good sign, but I was more worried about hitting against the top Cheetah pitchers for the first time. There would be no more predictable strike-zone fastballs from Coach Rizzuto.

In the first half inning, no balls were hit to me at third base. I was sixth in the batting order, so with only one bloop single and a walk from us hopefuls, I just missed getting an at-bat. In the top of the second inning I took an easy grounder and threw the runner out at first. I was happy with my performance, but it wasn't the kind of play that would wildly impress the coaches. I was the first to go up in the bottom of the second inning. The Cheetahs' lefty ace, Phil McDirvish, was pitching. Phil was notorious for throwing a scary curveball, the kind that goes straight for your head, then careens into the strike zone.

The first pitch: I was going to "take"—as in not swing—no matter what.

It was a fastball outside.

1 and 0.

I was ready to swing on the next pitch, but it was a blazing high one. I couldn't hold back and swatted at it, all arms and off balance.

1 and 1.

When Phil was ready, I raised my hand and stepped out of the box. I knew from Little League last year that this was when he liked to use his curveball. I took a couple of practice swings, stepped back in the box, and lifted my bat.

The ball came in spinning like the world, straight toward my right shoulder.

I steadied myself and waited for the break.

Within five feet of me, the ball swerved. I caught the ball early, nailing it over the first baseman's head. It landed just foul.

1 and 2.

With two strikes against me, I had to swing at anything that looked good. Phil would come in with something tricky. But what was tricky at this point: a curve or a fastball? At the last second, I decided it was going to be a curve.

I was right. The ball was a little low, heading inside, then it began to tail away from me. I stretched and swung. The end of my bat scooped the ball on the outside of the corner. It flew softly, well over Sherman's head at third. I ran to first base, rounded the turn to second, saw the ball coming in from left field, and returned to first. I had gotten my single.

"Nice at-bat, Darce-man," Ralph said, patting me on the back as I sat down on the hill. Ralph and I had planned to meet at the end of the tryout so that he could "prep me" for the date with Danalda. "Who knew that Phil was going to throw another curveball?"

"Good guess," I said, shrugging. "I hope it was enough."

"When do you find out?" he said carefully.

"Coach Rizzuto said we'll get a letter in the mail next week."

"Right," he said, pulling out his own folded piece of paper. "Well, listen. I gotta go meet Clark, a.k.a. Dracula, at the mall. We've got some lines to rehearse . . . and a couple of security guards to bug. Here. My brother gave me a little help with this."

He handed me the sheet.

"Thanks, Ralph," I said. "Wish me luck."

"Luck," Ralph said with a smirk. He hopped onto his bike and pedaled away.

THE WORD on Double-Dating at the Movies
by Ralph Peterson, Esq.
(with help from his brother, John Peterson)

Before the movie:

1. Watch out for the other guy. Don't get competitive or talk more to him than your date. No sports or stats, but be friendly with him. If he doesn't like you for some reason, you're dead.

2. Buy the tickets, the popcorn, and anything else. This is usually a flip of the coin, but I bet Danalda likes being treated.

3. Open a door for her once. If it goes over badly, make a joke of it and never do it again.

4. Buy popcorn with no topping. It's great for unslimy, accidental hand contact.

At the movie:

1. Get an outside seat if you can. Easy access to men's room mirror for personal pep talk.
2. Leave the armrest free. She will take it and then you can move in for some arm-to-arm contact. The first step in every successful movie date.
3. Don't hold her hand. That's for geeks and fourth graders. Putting your arm around her is the first big step. (DO NOT YAWN BEFORE PUTTING YOUR ARM AROUND HER. This move is older than Grandpa S, and so uncool.) One quick easy motion and it's done.
4. Once around the shoulder, you'll know where you stand. If she's tense and hasn't moved toward you, you are gonzo. Best to retreat to the washroom and cry. If she leans toward you, you're in business.
5. Next is the head move. Gently put your head against hers. Again if she doesn't move away, things are very good.
6. The head turn is a skill of a true master. Turn your head slightly toward her as if you are moving to kiss her. Hold position for a couple of seconds, then turn back. If on the third try she hasn't turned at all toward you, lift head away.

Plan B: Go back to 4 and move the hand that is around her. Shift in your seat to get started, pretending that your hand moved accidentally. Ideal spots: her neck, the top of her shoulder blade. Dead ends: the side of her arm and the back of her head.

7. If none of this works, you never had a chance in the first place.

R

When I finished Ralph's note, I felt sick to my stomach. For every rule, I had a thousand questions. It was worse than the official baseball rulebook. Way worse.

I was the first to arrive at Station and Third on Friday night. Ralph had said nothing about being unfashionably early, but already I knew it was a mistake. Five minutes later, Michael, Jennifer, and Danalda arrived together. They had apparently met on the way. Danalda waved to me, and Michael nodded and smiled. Jennifer quickly broke the ice.

"Ex-lab mate, you're here early," she said, giggling. "How'd the last tryout go?"

"Um . . . good. Yeah, fine."

"You gonna make the team?" Mike asked as we started walking along. He probably knew better than Danalda and Jennifer that my chances were small.

"Yeah, I hope so," I said. "I hit pretty well."

"Maybe you can strut your stuff next Sunday," he said. "Jennifer and I are organizing a just-for-fun game at the small diamond."

"Sure, sure," I said to him, but I couldn't stop thinking about the tryout. "I don't know about strutting my stuff, though. I mean, my hitting was pretty good, but I had a tough grounder in the third inning. Could have been an error."

"I can't *waaaaaait* for this movie," Danalda interrupted, nudging Jennifer. "I just love Shamus Welt. Talk about cheekbones."

Michael rolled his eyes at me over Jennifer's shoulder. I smiled back at him weakly, dropping my head. It was only two minutes in, and I was already failing to connect.

When we got to the theater, I made sure I got to the ticket booth first. When I handed Danalda the ticket, she giggled at Jennifer and Michael, who each paid for their own. In line at the snack bar, Jennifer was talking nonstop about Shamus Welt, and I somehow missed that Danalda didn't want any of the large popcorn I'd bought. Jennifer then tried to help by saying that she'd share it with me instead.

When we were walking down the aisle, Jennifer slowed me down for a handful of kernels, and Danalda sped ahead. It took everything I had to take the bag away from Jennifer's hand and to catch up with my date. I could do nothing about Michael stopping to look at the movie poster outside the theater. So I was soon stuck in a sandwich of two best friends.

More talk of movie stars pinned me to my seat between the two girls. Leaning over me was Jennifer, eating popcorn and talking. Danalda's "Do you think so?," "You are so right," "Yeah, like, in my dreams" kept Jennifer coming. Every once in a while, one of them would ask me a question, but it was like watching a superlong rundown between first and second base and then being asked to make a call.

Mike finally arrived, putting his hand on Jennifer's back and giving me a look, with his eyebrows raised. I had the strange feeling of being in a dream, like none of this was actually happening to me.

When the lights finally went out, I felt a cross between relieved and terrified. The armrest stayed empty beside me for the first half hour of the movie. Danalda did lean over once to whisper something to Jennifer, but then it was back to her hands-on-lap, upright pose. A couple of times, I snuck looks across at Danalda, her face flickering in the movie lights as she watched. There was absolutely no sign from her face whether she was concentrating on the film or waiting impatiently for me to make my move.

Meanwhile, Jennifer sure loved popcorn. Her hand was constantly fumbling for the bag as she watched the movie, engrossed. I knew I was supposed to feel happy about my situation, finally on a date with the girl of my dreams, but I felt slightly trapped.

And then suddenly, out of nowhere, Danalda's smooth hand slipped into mine, and Ralph's rules went out the window. I nearly jumped in my seat as our hands touched. I looked over slowly, but her eyes were still on the film. I squeezed a little to communicate, but nothing came back.

What now, Ralph? S.O.S. signals?

What I really needed was an on-date coach, someone to give me signs, a wiggle of the ear or a kick of the dirt. Ralph had said that holding hands was for geeks and fourth graders; meanwhile Danalda, one of the coolest girls in school, had me in a death grip.

My racing mind seemed to produce only one thing: sweat. My hand began to leak like our kitchen faucet, a constant flow from an unidentified location. But still Danalda didn't flinch. I didn't want to insult her by pulling away, but I felt something had to be done. Finally, something did happen—in the film—to make people jump. Danalda's hand loosened, and I slid mine away. Danalda looked over, but I couldn't bear to meet her gaze. What a disaster!

I noticed that Jennifer hadn't reached for some popcorn in a while and stole a glance left. Jennifer's head was hidden in Michael's shoulder.

While my hand dried off in the cool theater air, I charted my course. If I was going to get anywhere with Danalda, it would have to be soon. Finally, I did what Ralph had told me: my arm rose in one swift movement, like a half backstroke, but my elbow got caught on the back of the seat, and my hand was left dangling like a spider over her right shoulder. I couldn't tell if she knew my arm had moved, and I didn't want to scare her with my hand.

Someone behind Danalda cleared her throat. I closed my eyes and dropped my arm. Danalda jerked a little, but she quickly grabbed my right hand with her left. She then leaned her head toward me like Jennifer, and I moved in to do the same. I must have moved a little too suddenly. Our heads connected with a sound that only two skulls could make, a dull clonk.

"Ow!" Danalda said, looking up with one eye closed.

I could feel Jennifer's body shift beside me.

"Sorry," I whispered, leaning in.

Danalda's bluish-gray eyes were black in the theater, and as she looked at me, I had no idea what she was thinking. A second later, Danalda's soft lips were suddenly on mine. For the shortest moment, we kissed.

20

◆

SAFE OR OUT

◆

a call **def.** An umpire's decision on a pitch or a play.

"What do you mean, 'only for a couple of seconds'?"

It was 10:30 P.M. and I was in my room. Ralph had said his parents were out and I could call if I got home before eleven.

Ralph deepened his voice to sound official. "Well, you know what this means, don't you?"

"I know what what means?"

"You didn't really get to first base."

"What are you talking about? Of course I got to first base. First base is kissing—"

"Darcy, Darcy, Darcy," he said condescendingly. "Maybe in 1950, a little three-second smooch meant getting to first base. But today, it's got to be a full-on make-out. You know, swapping spit. Tongues and all." There was a pause. "So it was just one kiss at the movie. How did the date end? Did you even kiss her good-bye?"

"No," I said defensively. "After the movie, the four of us stepped out onto the street, talked for a bit, and then said good-bye. How was I supposed to kiss her in front of them?"

"Well, that's what it takes to get to first base. You have to take a big cu—"

"Ralph!" I yelled.

There was an angry silence.

"Listen, don't hang up on me or anything," he pleaded. "I didn't say you were thrown out!"

"How can I not be out if I didn't get to first base? Look," I said, trying not to get too worked up. "Forget it. I'm not going to hang up . . . but I gotta go."

"It's not the end of the world," he said, trying to backtrack. "I mean maybe you have three outs . . . maybe you have a whole game . . . maybe you have a whole seas—"

"I gotta go."

"But—"

"But nothing. Bye."

Ralph might be one of my oldest, best friends, but he wasn't my umpire.

On Monday morning, Danalda and Jennifer found me at my locker to ask what I was doing for lunch. Ever since the beginning of spring, the Cool Crowd had been hanging out at the bleachers, a specific spot on the rows of benches at the northern end of the field. As usual, Jennifer did all the talking. I was getting kind of sick of Jennifer always being around, but before I knew it, I'd agreed to meet the two of them at the bleachers at 12:10.

At noon, on the way to the field, I ran into Kamna. She had her clarinet case with her. I knew she had been doing extra practice for the upcoming music festival.

"Hey, stranger," I said.

"Hey," she said flatly, not stopping as she passed by.

"Wait," I said, turning toward her. "I've got some news."

"Darcy—"

"I did it! I got to first ba—"

"Darcy!" she almost screamed. She looked around quickly, and then she whispered, "Look. Hurray. Congratulations. You did it. Now, can I go?"

"Sure," I said, hurt. "I just thought—"

"No, Darcy, you didn't," she said. "Do me a favor and just stay away from me."

"But—"

"Can't you take a hint?" she said. "I gotta go."

I stood there completely confused for a minute. Finally I shrugged my shoulders and made my way outside.

Up in the bleachers with the Cool Crowd, I finally had some time alone with Danalda. For once, Jennifer had some other distraction—Andrea and Derrick had broken up over the weekend, and Jennifer elected herself chief consoler. Danalda and I found ourselves on the top bleacher, looking out over the field together. She put her hand in mine.

"So, that movie was good," I said. The truth was I couldn't remember anything about it.

"Yeah," she said. "Pretty good. Um . . . you're not friends with that girl, Camera, are you?'

"You mean Kamna?" I asked, surprised. "Yeah . . . sorta."

"Where is she from again . . . Geeksville?" she asked, giggling.

"No," I said, shocked. "London, England."

"Oh, right," she said.

There was an awkward silence.

"So, when's your first baseball game of the season?" she asked.

"Umm . . . I'm not sure . . . they haven't picked the team yet."

"Oh," she said. "But you're going to make it, though, right?"

"Um . . . I hope so," I said.

"Oh," she said again, letting go of my hand and fixing her hair.

"Did anyone ever tell you that you have a nice swing?" I said, trying to turn the conversation around.

"What do you mean?" she said, looking slightly annoyed. "I haven't played baseball for eons."

"I saw you in the fall at lunchtime," I said.

"Oh, that," she said. "That was stupid."

"No, it wasn't."

She made a scrunched-up face. "You're funny."

"Funny ha-ha, or funny weird?" I asked dolefully.

"See what I mean?" she said, and looked away.

We were silent until Michael jumped three bleachers toward us.

"Hey, man," he said, putting his hand out for a Cool Crowd handshake—a finger knuckle grip, ending with a light shoulder bump. "Wassup?"

"Not much," I said.

"Cool," he said. "You gonna come out for a little co-ed ball on Sunday?"

I looked at Danalda, who just shrugged at me indifferently.

"I guess so, sure," I said.

"Cool," he said again as Danalda got up without a word and skipped back down the bleachers.

Thelma found me at my locker at the end of the day.

"Whoa," she said. "Did you ever screw up!"

"What do you mean?"

"With Kamna!"

"What are you talking about? I did what she told me to do, and I was, like, successful. *We* were successful. I just wanted to share the good news."

Thelma shook her head and just stared at me.

"When Kamna first told me about the baseball and girls stuff," she said finally, "I thought she was crazy. 'What could Darcy possibly not understand about girls?' I said. Well, now I have my answer."

"What don't I understand?" I said.

"Everything," Thelma said.

"Like what?"

"I'm not going to spell it out for you, Darcy."

"Fine," I said. "I gotta go."

The next three days felt like the same one over and over. Hanging out with Danalda and the Cool Crowd, worrying about the baseball letter from Coach Rizzuto, and trying to forget about Kamna's yelling at me seemed to sap all my energy. On the bleachers, I focused on not sounding "funny" while Jennifer fussed over the team lists for the co-ed game. After school, I rushed home for the mail. On Wednesday, my heart jumped when I saw a white envelope for me, but I soon saw that it was a renewal form for my subscription to a baseball magazine. Waiting for the letter was as torturous as a delayed call from an umpire.

On Thursday night, I watched my first Major League Baseball game of the season. The Cincinnati Reds were playing the L.A. Dodgers. The Dodgers had this new pitcher on the mound, Bo Loller, who was a former outfielder turned knuckleballer. Loller was pitching a no-hitter when Del Anderson hit a line-drive single in the fourth inning. I gave a yelp for Loller's lost no-hitter, and Sam came running into the room.

"You okay in here?" she said. Beattie was out playing baseball and Nap was still at the college.

"Yeah, this new knuckleballer had a no-hitter going," I said. "Not anymore."

"Knuckleballer?" Sam said, wincing toward the TV. "I think I've heard that term before."

"Yeah, probably from Grandpa," I said. "He used to talk about this tricky pitcher named Al Zimer, but he was a spitball—"

"Darcy, don't joke," Sam said sharply.

"I'm not joking," I said, keeping one eye on the game. "Grandpa used to talk about him in the winter."

Sam was silent for a moment. Then she asked, "Grandpa used to talk about someone called Al Zheimers?"

"No, it was more like Al Zimer, with no *s*. Grandpa said he played with him back in the fifties. He said he was sneaky and he could never get a hit off of him."

Sam giggled as if holding back a hiccup.

"What?" I asked, still looking at the screen.

"I shouldn't laugh," she said, sitting down beside me. "Can you turn that off for a second?"

"Why?"

"Darcy."

"Okay," I said, flicking the TV off. "What?"

"It has really been too long," she said. "Grandpa has . . . well . . . we're not sure, but we think he might have a disease called Alzheimer's. That's why he started forgetting things, getting frustrated and mixing things up. They aren't sure, the doctors, I mean. But he does seem to be getting worse."

"Grandpa has a disease?" I said, feeling suddenly queasy.

"Well, we aren't really sure," she said. "When the doctor said it might be Alzheimer's, Grandpa nodded his head like he was expecting it, but then he kept on insisting he was fine. You know how stubborn Grandpa can get. I guess that's where the baseball metaphor came from."

"Baseball metaphor?"

"Yes, you know, your grandpa is notorious for his baseball metaphors, comparing life to a baseball game. I guess Alzheimer's became Al Zimer, some sneaky pitcher. He used to call me the Pinch Runner when your father and I first met. He said I wasn't going to stick around for long. I guess it's just Grandpa's way of dealing with things."

"You mean he's not mad at me?"

"Oh, Darcy," she said, reaching over. "Why would he be mad at you?"

When I tried to say something, tears welled up in my eyes. I shrugged.

"No one is mad at you," she said soothingly.

But I wasn't convinced.

21

◆

SCORING THE GAME

◆

official scorer **def.** The person who is responsible for watching the game and recording the game's statistics. He/she makes judgments on the events of the game, such as determining whether a fielding play is an error or not.

At school on Friday, after Spanish class, I saw Ralph in the hallway.

"You going to the co-ed baseball game on Sunday now that you've graduated to the Cool Crowd?" Ralph asked, trying not to sound jealous.

"I guess so," I said.

"Michael asked if I wanted to come, but I'm not so sure whether everyone—like Simone, for example—would want me there."

"You should come," I said, but I knew what he meant. "Try to forget all that stupid Cool Crowd stuff."

Ralph nodded uncertainly. "I got to get to class."

Ralph was nice enough not to ask about the Cheetahs. I was tense for the rest of the day about the letter from Coach Rizzuto. Over half the guys trying out had gotten word. I knew that Sherman Smith had made the team simply by the way he walked by me, smirking. When 3:30 came, I rushed out of school.

No one was home when I got there, but sitting on the table was a letter from Cherrydale Junior High. I dropped my backpack and whipped the letter off the table. I could barely breathe as I ripped open the envelope and slid the single folded piece of paper out. My eyes fell on the page, searching for the answer. "Thank you very much for . . ." My eyes scanned. ". . . after careful consideration . . ." and then finally, ". . . Unfortunately, you have not made the Cheetahs this season. Please come out again next year . . ." I dropped the letter back on the table, picked up my bag, and slunk into the den.

I don't know how long I sat in Grandpa's chair. Sam and Beattie got back home eventually. Sam jumped, startled, not expecting to see me there as she rushed through the den. Beattie asked if I wanted to throw the ball in the backyard, but I just shook my head. When Nap got home, the house was smelling like dinner. I heard him open the front door, and then imagined him flipping through the mail as usual. It seemed to take him longer to arrive in the living room. He walked into the den and pulled Grandpa's footrest up to sit on. In his left hand was my letter.

"Bad news," he said.

I nodded.

"I know how much this means to you, Darcy," he said softly. "You did your best. I know you did." He put his hands on his knees and sighed. "Is there anything I can do?"

"I want to see Grandpa tomorrow."

"Okay," he agreed. "We'll do that . . . Just you and me."

He sat there silently.

"How are . . . *other* things?" Nap finally said.

"Other things?"

"Look, I know we've already had the birds and the bees talk, Darcy," he said. "But when it comes to girls, well, my advice is that you should always go with your gut."

I was blushing and couldn't look him in the eyes.

"Well," Nap said, slapping his hands on his knees. "I should go see if your mother needs some help."

Dwight called after dinner. He already knew.

"Yeah, I heard that Drew made backup second and Charlie got backup short," Dwight said matter-of-factly in his high-pitched voice. "I knew Coach Rizzuto couldn't cover all the bases with backups. I heard that Charlie had some so-so tryouts, but somehow I knew they wouldn't ignore his big Little League stats from last year. What's a tryout for, though, if you can't prove yourself? Ridiculous. Anyway, Darce, you should be proud. You got a hit off of Phil and took it right to the wire. Hey, maybe you'll make it next year."

Later, Ralph called.

"That sucks, Darce-man," Ralph said. "You were robbed. You looked on fire out there when I saw you. Hey, just for that, I'm going to come to that stupid co-ed baseball game. To hell with the Cool Crowd. Maybe I should wear my old Little League uniform. That'd show them, eh, Darce!"

I laughed, but only for Ralph's sake. We didn't talk for long. Ralph made me promise I'd come to the game on Sunday. The truth was I couldn't fathom doing anything.

The next morning, Nap woke me up with my favorite breakfast: soft-boiled eggs with slices of toast for dipping. Nap explained that he'd called ahead so that Grandpa knew we were coming and that Beattie and Sam had gone to do some shopping before Beattie's game. Nap said it was going to be just "the Spillman Men." When we got to the Home, Nap insisted that I go in without him while he parked the car. I didn't mind. I wanted to break the news to Grandpa on my own. When I knocked and walked in, he was standing by the window, looking out.

"I like to watch the birds fight for a space on that wire over there." He pointed out to the right.

I moved toward him so that I could see. There were a couple of them there, not fighting, but looking off across the horizon together like friends.

"How's my boy doing?" he said, putting his hand on my arm.

"Not so hot, Grandpa," I said, sitting down on his bed.

"Why so glum? Did you get the thumb?" he said, sitting down beside me.

"Sort of," I said, looking up at him. "I didn't make the baseball team."

"Oh," he said, staring at me, starting to look confused. "Did you stay a step and a dive—"

"—from the line. Yeah, Grandpa, just like you said."

"How about your batting?"

"I did everything you told me. The pitcher, Phil, he's got this nasty curve, but I waited on it. I got a single."

"What went wrong, son?"

"I might have made an error. But I don't think so. It was close."

"Was it hard hit?"

"Yeah."

"Did you have to dive?"

"Yeah."

"Was there a strange bounce?"

"Yep," I said. "It popped up and hit the tip of my glove."

"That doesn't sound like an error to me," he said angrily. "Who was the official scorer? I'll have to track that fella down."

"No, Grandpa," I said. "It was just a tryout. There was no official scorer."

Grandpa's eyes were getting that lost look. I didn't want him to get angry again. "I proved you right about something, though," I said cheerily.

"Yeah," I continued, looking out the window. "You were right about baseball and love. I got to first base with this girl, Danalda, because . . . because I . . . I used a baseball metaphor like you. Yeah, I treated the whole thing like an at-bat, and I did it. You were right. You shouldn't be in this place. I was the one who forgot, not you. I was at the diamond and should have been home."

When I glanced over, I was shocked to see that silent tears were crawling down his wrinkly face.

"What's wrong, Grandpa? You were right. It was my fault."

Grandpa began shaking his head, the tears still falling. "No, no. I'm sorry. It wasn't your fault. I put too much pressure on you. I'm so sorry. I should have listened. You were right not to throw the ball."

"But Grandpa, I didn't—"

"You were such a bright boy. I shouldn't have been so hard on you. It wasn't your fault. You know I always loved you, don't you?"

"Yeah, but—"

I heard something behind me and turned around. Nap was standing in the doorway, streams of tears making his face glitter in the overhead lights. He was looking at Grandpa with tenderness. His eyes shifted to me. He smiled and slipped out.

"I know you did, Grandpa," I said. "I know you love me. Hey, Grandpa, could you tell me the story about how you and Grandma met at McSweeney's again?"

His eyes stopped producing tears. They gleamed suddenly alive.

"I sure can," he stated, patting a spot on the bed closer to him.

22

◆

THE STATS DON'T TELL THE WHOLE STORY

◆

baseball history **def.** The sport's past is filled with amazing, strange, heroic, even sad stories.

When we left the Home, Nap took me out for some ice cream at Kerrie's Dairy in Bayfield. As soon as we sat down with our ice cream, Nap began to tell a story.

"I need to tell you something," he began tentatively. "When I was nine years old, your grandfather made me join the Little League baseball team. I hated baseball, but I knew when to keep my mouth shut. I guess he just couldn't understand why I would rather hang out at Miller's swamp collecting insects. Maybe he thought I'd learn to love the game. Well, I didn't. I wasn't that good and I wasn't interested.

"Anyway, my team did well and we got into the playoffs. Grandpa got so excited. He made me practice every day to improve my hitting and fielding. He started talking about the next season as if it were a certainty. . . ."

"What happened?" I said, unable to touch my ice cream.

"Well, in our first playoff game, it was tied in the bottom of the last inning. Norman Duffy—you remember, the big kid—was on second and David Swenson was at bat. There were two outs. The ball was hit in my direction in the outfield. I stopped the ball, looked up, and saw that Norman was already rounding third. I picked up the ball, but instead of throwing it, I held on."

"But you're supposed throw it to the cut-off man right away," I told him, exasperated.

"I know, I know," he said. "Your grandpa was my baseball teacher, too."

He slowly scooped a spoonful of ice cream.

"This might be hard for you to understand, Darcy. I guess I didn't want to play the next year and I didn't see any other way of doing it. Your grandpa, everyone, was yelling at me to throw the ball but I didn't . . . couldn't. I finally threw the ball as hard as I could, but it wasn't even close. Norman scored, and they won the game."

"Whoa," I said in disbelief.

"Yeah, big whoa," Nap agreed. "Your grandpa didn't speak to me for a long time."

I didn't know what to say, which was okay, because he wasn't finished.

"When your mom and I had you, your grandpa was ecstatic. He got you a little bat when you were three."

"The blue plastic one."

"Yes, the blue one," he said, smiling. "He would toss the ball to you for hours. But your mom and I were worried. We thought with our combined genes, there was little chance you were going to be good at baseball, let alone enjoy it. We were wrong. You loved the game, you were good . . . and Grandpa got the little-boy baseball player he always wanted."

I started to protest, to say that Grandpa must have wanted him as he was, but Nap stopped me.

"I was always so glad that you and Grandpa got on so well," he admitted. "But . . . our relationship has always been a little strained. Until today, Grandpa had never said that he was too hard on me. He had never said sorry. He had never said that he . . . loved me."

Nap's eyes were beginning to well up. He took a big gulp to stop the tears from falling.

"Which brings me to us, and to Grandpa's sickness, Alzheimer's," he said, clearing his throat. "I'm sorry we didn't talk about this sooner. It has been confusing for all of us. We didn't want to alarm you without knowing for sure about his condition . . . But still, I'm sorry. It's time . . . It's time the Spillman men communicated better with each other." He paused. "We . . . I mean, I love you, Darcy."

"I know you do, Dad," I said, embarrassed. "I . . . love you, too."

We ate our ice cream silently for a bit.

"Sam told me about Al Zimer, the spitball pitcher," he said, finally smiling gently. "We've suspected for a while that he probably has this challenging disease. We still don't know. The doctors know the symptoms, but they can't test for the disease. Along with forgetting simple things like the names of things and people, Grandpa seems to be mixing you up with me. Just like he did today."

"I know," I said. "But he always talks to me about *me* at first."

"It can be that way," Nap said, nodding. "One moment he will be like good ol' gall-stoned Grandpa, sharp as a tack, then things—names, ideas, feelings—vanish or get mixed up. It is very hard on him. He knows he can't remember things he should be able to."

"Like when a word is on the tip of your tongue?" I asked.

"Yes, like that, but more often, and about more important things. And it will probably get worse. We are going to have to make sure we take care of him."

I felt a wave of guilt wash over me as I thought of my forgetting to come home for Grandpa. Nap must have read my face.

"Darcy Jonathan Spillman," he said, looking at me hard. "It was not your fault that we put Grandpa into the Home. We had already been planning for it for the end of term. But when he went walkabout, we realized that, for his safety, it was better for him—better for all of us—that he go there sooner."

"Not better for me," I said sadly.

"I know it's hard, Darcy," he said. "Even though we argue sometimes, I miss your grandpa, too."

"You do?"

"Of course. He's my dad."

It's easy to forget something as simple as that.

"Can we visit him again together, just you and me?" I asked.

"Sure."

"Next time, you go in first, okay?"

Nap hesitated, but quickly reached over and tousled my hair. "You got it, my favorite all-star third baseman."

23

◆

MAKING A CALL

◆

first-base coach **def.** The coach who stands beside first base and coaches the first-base runner.

I spent all afternoon watching the Royals vs. the Red Sox, but I was restless. I wanted to talk to someone. Someone who would get what I was talking about. Someone who would understand how I was feeling. Someone who would want to know me, the new me. The one who had a sick grandfather. The one who didn't make the Cheetahs. The one who was still crazy about baseball. I picked up the phone.

Amazingly, Kamna's mother didn't answer the phone.

"Hello."

"Hi, it's Darcy."

"Oh, hi," she said coldly.

"I just wanted to tell you that you were right about—"

"Hey, look," she interrupted. "Whatever you do is none of my—"

"—about my grandpa. We think he has that disease you told me about, Alzheimer's."

"Oh," she said, suddenly soft. "I'm so sorry, Darcy."

Her voice made my throat tighten. I bit my lip.

"I also didn't make the Cheetahs."

"Oh, Darcy," she said again. "I'm really sorry."

"I'll live," I said, swallowing my tears away like Nap. "It's not the end of the world."

"No, it's not," she said kindly. "But it's very important. Is there anything I can do?"

"I don't know, I—"

All of a sudden, I heard someone speaking loudly to Kamna in the background.

"Sorry," she said. "One sec."

I heard muffled talk, and then she uncovered the phone.

"I'm really, really sorry, Darce," she said, whispering. "I gotta go. My dad is forcing me to go to a cricket game at Bayfield Downs all day tomorrow. He knows I'm the only one who can't say no. Talk to you Monday, okay?"

"Sure," I said sadly.

I sat there for a while, staring at the TV, not taking in the game. Somewhere in my sorrow, there was something positive, a tiny bit of happiness. Like some good news you've just heard, but for the life of you, you can't remember what it is.

Beattie and I watched the end of the Royals–Red Sox game together. She was still in her uniform from her game that morning, and she didn't say anything as she flopped beside me on the couch. Because the sun always came strongly through the TV-room windows in the late afternoon, I had closed the shutters. The two of us were sitting there watching the game in the dark.

"We lost today," Beattie finally said at a commercial.

"Oh," I said, still looking at the TV. "Too bad."

"Dwight's an annoying umpire," she stated.

"I bet he's good, though."

"Yeah, I guess," she agreed. "He told me you didn't make the Cheetahs . . . but I knew anyway. Even if no one told me. No one tells me anything around here."

The game came back on, and we were silent for a while.

"Danalda Chase is not your type," she said suddenly.

"What do you mean, not my type? How would you know about Danalda?"

"Um, like, I'm a girl, if you hadn't noticed," she said. "Even though she seems nice and quiet on the outside, I think all she really cares about is being cool. Danalda's definitely not your type."

"You mean I'm not in her league," I said sourly.

Beattie was silent for a moment. The Royals center fielder, Brent Pearson, hit a hard single to left field. When he arrived at the base, he took off his batting glove and stuffed it in his back pocket while the first-base coach talked in his ear.

"No, Darcy," she said in a voice that I'd never heard. "*She's* not in *your* league."

When I woke up the next day, I figured I'd go to the co-ed baseball game at the small diamond. When I arrived at the park gate just after noon, both teams were abuzz in the fenced-in dugouts. I ambled along the third-base line to the nearest team. It looked like Ralph had elected himself captain, as he was organizing the boy/girl/boy/girl lineup. Someone said something to him, and he swerved around with a smile.

"Spillman, our big hitter," he announced like he was onstage. Everyone looked over, and my eyes fell. "What took you so long?" he said, more quietly. "You're on our team, the Already Victorious, and you're hitting cleanup after Karen."

I nodded while scanning the other side for Danalda. She was there, behind the fence, but she was trying to say something to Michael, who appeared to be the coach of the other team. Ralph then announced that we were taking the field first. Everyone ran out to their positions, and Ralph grabbed me gently by the arm.

"You don't look so hot," he whispered. "You okay?"

"Yeah," I said, feeling calm. "I'm fine."

Brenda Stout had taken third base—actually all of the infield positions had been taken. There were too many players in the outfield, but that was the only place to go. I found an opening behind shortstop at mid-outfield and waited. It felt strange not being at my regular station at third, but somehow good. The ballpark was littered with our fielders, but the other team—dubbed "In the Bag"—still scored three runs. Danalda did not get up, but Jennifer hit a dribbling single that the pitcher, Greg, did not try hard enough to get. I didn't mind—I wasn't in the mood for a serious game of baseball.

I tried to catch Danalda's eye a couple of times, but she had the sun in her eyes and a grimace on her face. Finally, we got a line-out double play orchestrated by none other than Sherman Smith, who was playing second. I said, "Nice play," to him as we walked in, but he pretended not to hear.

Ralph patted me on the back as I returned to the dugout and reminded me that I was hitting cleanup. It wasn't until the first batter, Andrea, hit a groundout to third that I noticed who was on first. It was Danalda.

Brett hit a double to right field, and then Karen struck out on four strikes—she was given an extra one, after three in a row. I stepped up to the plate with more butterflies in my stomach than my last tryout with the Cheetahs.

I popped the first outside pitch foul along the third-base line. 0–1.

The second pitch was way outside.

1–1.

The next pitch the ball looked juicer than a melon. I swung hard and hit it high and hard, but way foul.

1–2.

I was planning on really smacking the next pitch, but then I held back. I swung late and slapped it safely into left field and sauntered to first base. My stomach was tight with nerves as I arrived. Danalda smiled uncomfortably, and I forced one back.

"Hi," I said.

"Hi," she replied, looking down at the ground.

Lisa swung for a strike.

"I didn't make the Cheetahs," I said.

"Yeah," she said coldly. "I know."

"Oh well," I said. "Maybe next time."

Danalda just shrugged and looked away.

Lisa fouled one back into the backstop.

I looked down at third base. There was no third-base coach. I looked over my shoulder. There was no first-base coach.

I looked over at Danalda and swallowed.

"Danalda?"

"Yes?"

"I don't think we should date anymore," I said.

The world seemed to shake with the beat of my heart.

"I agree," Danalda said, her face going red.

Lisa took a big cut and completely missed the ball.

Three out.

Danalda walked up to me and put her hand on my arm. "I'm sorry to have to dump you like this. I didn't want to hurt you, but it's just not working out."

She glided by without a word, and I stood there in disbelief. Finally, I strode toward our dugout.

"What's going on?" Ralph said as I approached.

"I've got to go," I replied.

"But you—" he said, stopping mid-sentence.

He stared at me for a moment, and then we both looked over to the group of girls huddled around Danalda in the other dugout.

He patted me on the back and said, "You know best, Darceman. Give me a call later on." Then he turned back to the team and yelled in typical Ralph Peterson fashion, "Let's play ball."

As I walked away from the diamond, I actually felt relieved. I thought about what Danalda had just done and smiled to myself. I didn't care what anyone thought. For the first time in a long time, I was doing something different: I was going with my gut.

24

◆

STRIKING OUT
ON YOUR OWN

◆

a whole new ball game **def.** When a game or situation
changes dramatically.

The bus to Bayfield arrived right as I got to the stop. I found
a single seat, opened a window, and took a deep breath. As I
closed my eyes, the wind swept across my face. I must have nodded off, because the bus jerked me awake just as we pulled in
front of the stop by Grandpa's Home. I glanced at the familiar
brown bricks of the building, took another deep breath, and
then looked away.

The bus felt even jerkier as it pulled away, passing unfamiliar
intersections and stopping when I wasn't ready. I had only been
to Bayfield Downs once for a sixth-grade cross-country meet.

The only thing I knew was that you could only get to the Downs from Bayfield Road—the road we were on—by a wooded, hilly trail that ended beside the field. It was going to be a few more minutes before the bus got to the beginning of the trail.

When I finally arrived at the Downs, I found myself behind the bleachers that circled the field. I could see the backs of cricket fans as they watched. I walked through an opening between sets of bleachers. I saw that many of the fans were holding rolled-up programs, and I heard the buzz of their conversations about numbers and plays that I did not understand. I looked over at the players all dressed in white and scattered around the circular field, and thought that from above they would look like a constellation of stars.

After I searched for a while, rounding the inside, looking up at the bleachers, I saw them. Kamna and her father were sitting at the top, watching the match. Her father, with his bushy gray eyebrows and slick, parted hair, was looking seriously across the pitch, saying something to his daughter every once in a while. I could already see from his furrowed brow and intense black eyes that Kamna's father was going to be hard to win over—it was going to take more than just one cricket game.

Kamna saw me just as I reached their level. At first, she showed a flicker of surprise and moved to put a warning hand on her father's arm, but she stopped. She waited for a moment, and her face broke into a smile. I grinned back at her, comfortable, awkward, and terrified. As I stepped toward Kamna and her father, I remembered something. It was that small bit of happiness, the thing I was having trouble remembering just a day before.

It's still something that's hard to name, but I know how it feels. It feels like Ralph nailing his first line on opening night and Dwight calling the final strike in the junior girls' playoffs. It feels like Sam, smiling her confident smile, telling me that everything will be all right. It feels like sitting in the darkness watching baseball with Beattie, and hearing her say that I am more than I ever thought I was. It feels like Nap rubbing the top of my head like he hasn't done in years. It feels like Grandpa Spillman, smiling at me with knowing eyes, patting the spot beside him and inviting me to listen to the story about how he fell in love. It feels like playing within yourself and going with your gut, even if, in the end, things don't always turn out the way you thought you wanted.